Takeoff:

Seeing Beyond

the Clouds

A work of fiction

By: Austin Jackson

To Mayor Avery
Thanks for supporting
Takeoff

First Printing, 9/16/2014

ISBN 978-1-312-52517-7

Austin Jackson can be contacted regarding any inquiry of the book at:
www.takeoffsbc.wix.com/real

Special acknowledgement to my parents, Emanuel and Tottie Jackson for their words of wisdom and encouragement. It has been a long road to get here, but they have been there with me all the way.

Takeoff:

Seeing Beyond the Clouds

Prologue

"Roger that Atlanta Center, Dal 302 is at flight-level 2-6-0 descending for 1-5- thousand."

Austin looked over at his co-pilot, "Alright Dan, 1-5- thousand."

"Captain!" Dan shouted. "The knob's not responding!"

"What do you mean?"

"The altitude hold, it's not responding!"

"I don't understand." Austin said with determination and confusion in his eyes. "Contact air traffic control Dan."

Austin stared at the plane's controls. He scanned left and right then picked up the emergency procedure manuals. Austin flipped from page to page; his eyes scanned back and forth across the pages. "Anything?" Dan yelled. Austin replied without looking up, "Uh… no… not yet" he said frowned. *"Brrriiinnngg!"* The cockpit phone rang. Austin, in hopes this would provide answers, grabs the phone. "Yeah- Go ahead Jenna!" "There's a burning smell coming from the lavatories captain." She said. "Gotcha Let's figure something out *real fast*, and I'll call you right back." He hung the phone up and looked at Dan. By now, Dan's forehead was moist, his brow was stern and his eyes were fixated on the Altitude hold. "Dan." Austin said, "We have a smoke smell in the back."

"Oh my gosh." Dan whispered. A smoke smell on a plane is a pilot's nightmare. The atmosphere was absolute chaos, but it was strangely calm.

At that moment, the Master Caution Warning light lit up and a loud buzzer went off through the cockpit; surely those first class passengers could hear it. Suddenly the instruments started to glitch. They flickered on and off. The Buzzer was getting louder, or so it seemed. "DAN LET TOWER KNOW WE'LL NEED LANDING PRIORITY!" Dan picked up the radio, and pressed the side button. "Atlanta Center Dal 302 is at-"

"Dan it's off." Austin interrupted. He gripped the flight yoke, or what some may call the steering wheel.

"What? How can it be off?"

"The Avionics are off. We just lost the GPS."

Dan reached over and grabbed the avionic switch. He flipped it up and down. "Nothing." Austin said. "So we have no way to talk to ATC?" he continued.

"I guess not."

"Well we're coming down one way or another."

"Yeah we're gonna have to do a visual approach." Dan said.

"Ok, get the map right there. Find us an airport-Last check we were two miles away from that one right there." Austin pointed at the map. The instruments stop flickering and a fast-falling number caught his attention. "Dan..." Dan looked up. "Dan we're losing fuel!" Austin started sweating.

It was three different pilot nightmares all piled into one. *Everything* was going wrong. "Let me get my calculator." Austin mumbled. He reached behind him and into his black suitcase. He tapped on the calculator, glancing up periodically to look at the fuel meter. "Dan we have about ten minutes of fuel left."

"No Austin! Can't be! Look how much we have left." The Master Caution light illuminated again. The buzzer followed. Austin tapped the button to turn off the buzzer saying, "Look how fast we're losing fuel! HEY Call Jenna back. NO! YOU FIND US A PLACE TO LAND, I'll call Jenna. He picked up the phone. "No dial tone Dan!" Austin grabbed the yoke and pushed it forward- throwing the plane downward. "Alright Captain, we have an Airport. It's an Air force base. Looks like our only option." Dan said.

"Dan, look..." The fuel meter, which told the number of pounds of fuel left in the tanks, showed 4 then 3 then 2 then 1 then 0. "We are officially out of fuel Dan." The engines died. The roar of the engines was now missed as complete silence filled the plane.

"Starting the RAT fan." Dan proclaimed. They believed that starting a fan that would give them a little bit of power, would be enough to land the plane safely.

"Austin we're coming down a little steep here..."

"I don't have control." He pulled the flight yoke up, pushed it in, turned it left and turned it right.

"Come on man pull up!"

"Can't! I'm trying!" He glanced up. "The hydraulic pressure is completely gone. We have no hydraulics." At that moment, it seemed that everything was going in slow motion. All Austin could see was his family's face-his beautiful wife and adorable children. All he could think about is what his death would do to them. He turned his head glancing out of the window. The trees that reminded him of his daughter's play set now looked full size and very close, almost unreal. The plane was just hundreds of feet from the ground, and seconds from crashing. Austin reached behind him and opened the cockpit door and yelled, "BRACE FOR IMPACT!"

BOOM! The plane hit the ground harder than can be imagined. It slid, clipping trees along the way. The Passengers screamed- children cried-adults cried as the plane rocked violently back and forth ripping across the ground of the woods. Once the plane stopped, there was another silence. This one was eerie and sounded like death. Austin could only see in a blur. Dan's head was leaning over to the right-bleeding and not moving. Austin, with gashes on his face, and what must've been broken arm, began to black out. His vision became spotty, and cloudy. All he could hear was a voice whispering to him. The voice said, "Make your mark on this world; accomplish everything that you are supposed to accomplish." It faded out, as his conciseness did.

In the hospital Austin was rushed into a room. The nurse tried to talk to him, but he couldn't hear her. Once the paramedics left the room the only sound that could be heard was the heart monitor. Beep-beep-beep BEEEEEEEEEEEEEEEEEEEEEEEEEEEEEPP. "We're losing him! Hand me the AED!" the nurse yelled. The doctor ran in. Another nurse handed him the automated external defibrillator. The doctor yelled, "CLEAR!" a pulse of energy went through Austin's body. His chest jerked upward and he could hear that voice again, it was a soft yet stern voice- it had the smoothness of a baby's bottom, and the sharpness a red rose thorn. "Make a difference" it said, "Change someone's life, because if you don't... then you're wasting your time." The voice faded away once more. "Again!" the doctor announced, "CLEAR!" "Beep-beep-beep-beep- BEEEEEEEEEEEEEEEEEEEEP!" Went the heart monitor. "MAN, IT'S LIKE THIS GUY HAS THREE HEARTS!" The doctor yelled. Suddenly there was a bright light and a whoosh of air. It was wet and cold- powerful, yet peaceful.

Austin woke up at home, on the floor of his parent's single bedroom apartment on the south side of Atlanta- in a cold sweat. His mom was passed out on the couch, probably on one of her drinking binges. Austin, getting grips of his surroundings, peeked out of the blinds. There was a man. He pointed a gun at a little boy, around Austin's age. The boy and Austin's eyes met for a moment. The boy's eyes begged for help, but in this neighborhood, jumping into something that was none of your business can get you killed, so he just observed from the window. The boy pointed Austin out to the gunman. Austin instantly shut the blinds and dropped to the floor. Moments later he heard a very familiar sound, "POW POW POW." The boy had been shot. Austin saw the shooter but wouldn't dare tell the police who it was out of fear of the shooter's friends. He was helpless and breathing heavily. It had seemed that the shooting triggered something in him. His inner greatness. He took a deep breath, gathered his thoughts and closed his eyes, for some reason not going to sleep though; for what seemed like the entire night, he mumbled to himself, rattled by what he saw and heard in his sleep, while repressing the emotions he felt from the boy being shot and fighting the delirium coming down on him. He said, "Can't...... can't make... a difference... if... "He would blink slowly, and continue, "If I'm asleep." Austin repeated this for about an hour. He was sure that he needed to get out of that neighborhood, or at least change it. He was determined to stay awake, shaken by fear, but it was a battle that was ultimately lost.

Perhaps this was the creation of a monster, or perhaps the creation of something great, that no one would understand. Perhaps this was the making of a new generation- one that Austin would lead, and march to greatness, where he could be remembered forever, or perhaps this was simply the beginning of the end.

Chapter 1

This story begins on the south side of Atlanta, about 30 minutes from the city center. It was a beautiful day. The skies were the perfect shade of blue, the cloud were like little cotton balls, and they just glided through the air with such grace.

Beep beep beep was the sound of his alarm clock. It startled him. "Uh, that alarm clock," he said, "I have got to fix that, I can't stand that noise." He reached over and turned the alarm clock off. Rolling over to the other side of the bed he said, "Good Morning!" no one answered. "Uh? Ashley?" he asked. He stepped out of the bed and paced the floor in his gym shorts "Ash?" He asked. "Where are you? Ashley?"

"I'm down stairs" She replied after a few moments. "Come down here."

"Ok, hold on, let me get ready for work; I'll be right down." He walked into the bathroom, and stared at himself in the mirror. He looked at himself with this smile, a smile so bright it could light up an entire room. He loved his job. Ever since he was six he wanted to be a pilot. For the past week he would look at himself in the mirror every morning, and smile, he recently had some dental work done, and the dentist told him to flush his gums with a substance in a needle. So he would smile to make sure everything was exactly how it should be. It must've felt good to wake up and not feel like he was going to work, but going to do something he loved. Austin grabbed his tooth brush and started brushing his teeth, then joyfully climbed into the shower. He was living the dream, and he knew it.

Out of the shower and dry, Austin reached for his white shirt and stuck his name tag to it. Then attached his gold bars to the shoulders of the shirt. He pulled his favorite black tie from his closet, wrapped it around his neck and tied it tight. After putting on his freshly pressed black pants and socks, he walked casually down stairs to see his wife. "Hey." He said walking up to kiss her. "Good Morning Captain." She said. They kissed.

"It smells good Ash, what'd you cook?"

"I made some from-scratch pancakes…"

"From scratch? Look at you!"

"Yes honey- and some thick cut bacon…"

"Oooweee! It sounds delicious. Where are the kids?" He said taking a seat.

"So where are you off to today?" She said ignoring his question and making him a plate.

"London."

"Oh wow, that should be fun." She said optimistically.

"Yeah, it's about a twelve hour flight, so that part I'm dreading." He said with a chuckle.

"So how long are you gonna be gone this time?"

"We leave today, stay in London for four days, and come home on the fifth day."

"Ok. Alright well I'm going to miss you." She said to Austin giving him the plate.

"Don't worry, I'm taking two weeks off after this trip, so I'll be around the house so much you'll be tired of me." He said reassuringly.

"Ok. Oh yeah, before I forget, you've been getting a lot of letters from different people."

"What do you mean?"

"Like, this one," She opened an envelope she found in the mailbox. "It says, 'Dear Mr. Jackson, I am very interested in your program. My son is very troubled. He's not coming home on time; he's being rude, and very disrespectful. I really think that a

program like this will change his life for the better…"
She stopped reading. "What Program babe?"

"Oh Yeah, Ash I forgot to tell you, I want to start
a Non-Profit organization."

"Ok." She said reluctantly, "*Now* this is kind of
making sense." Ashley chuckled. For the most part,
Ashley was pretty understanding. She never took
anything *that* seriously, and rarely made a big deal
out of anything. "So what's this organization about
exactly?"

"I don't really know, honestly. I just want to reach
someone and help somebody." Ashley nodded and
rubbed his back. "You know what I'm saying Ash? I
just want to make a difference. I learned a long time
ago that if you don't make yourself relevant, than
you're not important. Like, ok, think about this, what
would make me be in a history book today? Right
now? Nothing! Just getting up, and going to work is
not enough to make a difference."

"I get it." Ashley said. "I do, I get it. I think that
it's actually a great idea. And you know what, my

company, Dance Stars, will be one of your biggest contributors."

"Seriously?" He asked.

"Of course. You're my husband, and I will support you in everything that you do. Always remember that baby, I love you, and I got your back."

"Love you too." He grabbed her by the waist and they danced side to side. "You know getting through flight school was hard." He dipped her. "Seriously, it was really hard; it was hard as *He*....Hey! Hey kids." The kids ran to Austin, interrupting their parents.

"Where are you going daddy?" The six years old asked.

"Well Jordan I'm going to London today." He picked Jordan up. "Now, I'll be back in about a week, so you take care of your sister, and your mom ok?"

"Ok." Jordan said with a smile on his face. He admired his dad so much. He probably thought that Austin hung the moon in the sky.

"Oh, and before I forget, I'm going to take you fishing this weekend ok? You've never been fishing before right?" Jordan shook his head. "Ok good, I didn't think so. Then we are going this weekend when I get home." Jordan's face lit up.

"Mommy, did you hear that! I'm going fishing!" Jordan announced to his mother, as Austin turned to his daughter.

"Now Mia, same goes for you. Be good. Do your chores, and look after your brother." The 12 year old stared at her father. It was an icy stare– her arms crossed and full of attitude. She walked away. "What's her problem?" Austin said.

"Oh calm down baby, she just at that age where everything upsets her, and she's mad about everything."

"I thought we had at least 5 years until that attitude kicked in?"

"Don't worry, I'll talk to her." Ashley stopped talking and looked out of the kitchen window, where she saw one car in the driveway. "Hey, Austin, where's my car, I meant to ask you that?"

"Well, about that, I kind-of sold it."

"What! How could you sell my car- and without even telling me, that's so inconsiderate!"

"Calm down Ash, you'll get a better one. I promise."

"Alright, I'm holding you to that. Now what am I supposed to drive? How are you just gonna go on and sell *my car*?

"I got you baby, a buddy of mine is going to bring my car home as soon as I get to the airport, and I'll take a cab when I come home."

"But why? Why did you sell it?"

"I needed the money for some bills I've got to pay, and you know I'm trying to start this organization and all. I'll get you a better one."

"Whatever. I've learned to trust you, so I'll sit back as much as I can and let you do what you have to do, *for now.*" She mumbled, reluctantly accepting her car's fate. She turned her attention back to her daughter. "Well I'd better talk to that little girl before you do."

He leaned in to kiss her, "Love you! Jordan you be good, and take care of your sister."

"See you babe. You are going to call me every day right?" Ashley asked worried that she may never hear from him again. This was a pilot's wife's worry.

"Of Course; Matter fact, I'll video chat you." Ashley chuckled. Austin walked out of the door. Ashley flagged him down, "AUSTIN! AUSTIN!" She runs up to him. "Hey, you forgot something." She pulls from behind her back Austin's semi- automatic pistol. He quickly took it from her- looking around suspiciously and said, "Thanks" with a smile. He hopped in his 2001 sedan kicking some syringe needle under the seat, put the pistol in the glove compartment and left. Ashley stood there as he pulled off- smiling. He was her Prince Charming. She hadn't even noticed the needles, even though he just hid them right in front of her. She stood there for a while, watching Austin drive down the street, smiling. She sighed while smiling.

Jordan's Journal:

Today my dady left for London and he He is
gona come back and, and, yeah, we gona go fishing!
And I never been fishing! So I'm excited

Mia's Diary:

My dad is gone again. Who knows when he'll be back this time. He's left my mom alone again, probably to go off to London with his other family. He doesn't care about us. If he did he'd be here. He doesn't care about us. I heard on tv that when dad's leave they go all around, and do fun stuff with other families, but it's not fair. It's not fair that he would leave us to go with another family! It's just not fair, but he must not love me. That's my dad, I'm soo proud. ☹

Chapter 2

Austin walked through the airport. He just passed the security check point with his suit case casually behind him- a smile on his face, hat on his head, four gold stripes around his blazer sleeves- he's living his dream. "Hey Suzie" Austin said "Hey Austin." she replied. "Hey How ya' doing, Captain Jackson?" a fellow pilot asks. "Good Morning! I'm doing well, how about yourself?" before the other pilot could reply, a little boy ran up to Austin. "Hi are you a pilot?" The boy asked.

Austin replied, "Yes I am. What's your name?"

"My name is River."

"Hi River. Come on, let's walk and talk, I have a flight to catch." A lady walked behind River, making sure he didn't get into trouble I'm sure.

"Hi River's mom how are you?"

"I'm great." River's mom said, "He's always been so fascinated with planes- ever since he was a baby, and I just think that aviation is just incredible."

"So where are you guys going today?"

"London!" said River.

"Ok, cool, you guys are going to be on my flight then. Are you flying Dal Airlines?"

"Of course, they are the best!" River's mom said.

"Good, then you guys are gonna be with me." They walked up to the departing gate. The plane that they would be flying on today could be seen out of the window. Tons of children were crowding the gate's window. "Ok, you guys wait here. We're gonna go and plan the flight alright? We're gonna go make sure everything's good to go, and I should be back out to talk to you guys." Austin left the boy with his mother. A man dressed in black sat behind River and his mother. The man squinted his eyes at Austin as he sat. While walking to the flight planning room, just steps from the departing gate, Austin turned around to look at the boy. River was looking back at him, staring. Austin focused on the boy, not the creepy man sitting behind him. River had an admiring stare, the kind of stare that every young boy gives when he sees his favorite football player, or a firefighter or father. This really seemed to be a great start to Austin's spring morning. He took his Dal employee card out of his pocket and swipes it into the alarm system. The door clicked and unlocked and he walked in. "Good morning everyone! How are you all doing?" "HEY!!! CAPTAIN JACKSON!" everyone cheered. Austin sat down and pulled out a pen from his black suitcase.

"Alright, let's get to work." He said. Everyone sat. "Ok, so we're going to London today, do we have all of our Oceanic charts? Oh boy, anytime we have to cross the Atlantic, it's just tons of paperwork. So all our paper works' in order? We have our SID don't we?"

The first officer shook his head. "You know that they're gonna change it anyway. I mean goodness, we can't keep a standard instrument departure that *we pick* to save our lives."

"Ok, so which one do you all want to do? What do you think about this one?" Austin pointed at a map. Everyone nodded their head. "So it looks like we'll be going up to 39,000 feet." The first officer interrupts Austin, "Captain, I want you to meet somebody."

"Hey how ya' doing" Austin said shaking the man's hand.

"This is our second officer Ron O'Conner. " Dan continued.

"Good to meet you Ron."

"Sir, it's a privilege and an honor to meet you. I've heard a lot about you around the airport- you're very well known."

"Oh really?" Austin said in genuine disbelief. "Well, it's good to have you on board. This should be a pretty smooth flight, other than that turbulence around 2,100 feet."

After the flight had been planned, the flight crew relaxed and socialized before their nearly twelve hour flight. Some talked and laughed, some drank coffee and ate donuts, the rest just relaxed and texted on their phones.

"John Paul, are you ready for this flight?" The first officer asked.

"YEEEEESSSS honey YEEEESSS! I need some time away. I am so excited to get out of here!"

"Cool, cool, well like Captain said, it really should be a smooth flight crossing the Atlantic."

"YEEESS that's exactly what we need is a smooth flight. I am so tired of turbulence." He said sashaying to the coffee bar. He continued, "You know I don't really understand what it is about turbulence that is so scary... We have to deal with kids crying, adults crying, people vomiting, I mean it's just some rough air." He said with a flip of his hair.

"Is that Tamara back there hiding? Hey!" Austin said.

"Hey Captain- haven't worked with you in a while!"

"I know right. You know, *we all* have never worked on the same flight before- not *all* of us."

Tamara agreed, "That's true."

"So this should be an interesting flight today *honey*." John Paul said to the crew.

"So Dan are we looking at a certain STAR?" Austin asked.

"I mean, I don't like the one we have now, but as it stands we will do the Standard Terminal Arrival Route for… that one right there." The first officer pointed at a map. The door opens.

"Hi everyone!" She said. "Sorry I'm late; my flight was delayed in Denver." Austin stood up.

"Hi I'm the Captain, Austin Jackson."

"Hi, I'm Jackie." Austin looked down at her employee badge, conveniently placed on her chest, "Jackie Blake? That's a cool name. I thought it was gonna to say Robinson, but Blake is a cool name too." They chuckled.

"It's funny Captain Jackson, I've always wanted to work with you- they say that you are a lot of fun."

"Is that what they say?" Austin said. "I try to make the flight experience as fun as possible, because it's very stressful on us- the flight crew. I like how you all are all fun and stuff, I've worked with some really mean and hateful flight attendants. We're gonna have fun." Jackie walked to her seat, while Austin turned to face the crew. So are you guys excited to be going to London? I know you are John Paul," The crew chuckled. "But seriously, what are we gonna do when we get there? Like seriously, I've never been there and had a lot of time to kill, so I don't know what we should do? Every time I go to London, it's a turn and burn kinda thing, it's not like I get time to actually see some things, or go some places while I'm there." They laughed. "So what do y'all want to do?"

"I say let's go to the museums and check out some of the art while we are there." Tamara suggests.

Jackie said, "What about the food, are they *really* known for their food?"

"Well, I want to go shopping while we are there," John Paul added.

"Ok John Paul, we'll check out some stores. What about you Dan?" First officer Dan never really liked London much. He swears it's where he lost his favorite shirt, and lucky belt. Dan just shook his head. "Come on Dan, you know you want to go shopping and buy you something new. Now Dan, we've been friends for years, and I've seen your closet." The crew laughed. "So don't pretend that you don't like buying new things!" Austin continued. Dan smiled and replied, "I guess I'll go, plus I want to get y'all off my back."

Austin's phone rang. "Excuse me guys let me take this." He stepped into the corner of the planning room. "Hello?" he said. There were moments of silence. The crew was listening. "Uh sure. Of course. Ok-ok, so how much would this building cost? Ok. So the building is gonna cost…. Uuumm. Ok, well… I would have to talk that over with my wife. Of course- absolutely, so look, just send me an email, with all of that information on there. I'm actually on my way to London right now, so when I get back in town, we will definitely come by and take a look at that. Alright… Bye now." He turned around. The crew was completely silent, staring back at him. "Ok, you guys it's time to get on the plane. We have to go."

The crew walks out of the planning door and onto the jet-way, which connected the airport and the plane, but Austin stops and turns to go talk to the boy, River. River ran to Austin and the mysterious man in black stood up. Austin said, "Hey River, we have to go get the plane ready, so I'll see you on board ok?" "Ok Captain." River said. Austin walked back to the jet-way to get onto the plane. I think that

River calling him Captain really warmed his heart. This is what he worked so hard for so many years for-for that moment. Austin didn't grow up with much. His father was an engineer, but wasn't paid well. His mom struggled with her alcoholism and could never keep a job, making it twice as hard for him to get into flight school. In flight school he met Dan, some odd 20 years ago. River took him back to his childhood. And what some might see of his childhood as nothing, was traumatic to Austin. He walked onto the plane. "Hi Jenna." He said sarcastically. "Why weren't you in our briefing this morning?"

"I just got here, and it's been such a rough morning…"

"Ummhuum alright Jenna. Where's the relief crew?"

"In the back putting their things away."

"Let me go brief them really quickly, they must've been running late this morning." Austin walked to the back of the plane to brief the relief pilots. Jackie and Tamara were in one of the galleys prepping the cabin for the passengers. "What do you think that that phone call was about?" Jackie said.

Tamara said, "I don't think it was anything important."

"Naw girl, that could be something juicy. You don't think that Captain's having an affair do you? Woo! I see why people like working with him- and we still got twelve hours of drama to go! I love it *girl*, Love it!"

"Calm down. He mentioned his wife in the phone call."

"Yes girl! Have you never read the *pimps and playa's handbook*? You always check with the wife to see if he'll be able to make one of their, *appointments*."

"See, you are just being messy. Captain is a good man, known him for years."

"Well, I just met him, and, I know that you saw the way he looked at me."

"That's the look he gives to everyone Jackie. *Shh* here he comes!"

Austin asked, "You all doing good? Any problems or anything?"

They both nodded. "Everything is great Captain."

"Good." He said. He walked back up to the first class cabin on his way to the cockpit. "Austin!" Jenna whispered.

"That's *Captain* to you Jenna." He said laughing. "What's up?"

"Nothing much. How's your wife? How's Ashley?"

"She is great, she actually asked about you the other day. She said that your little girl is doing great in dance."

"Really?"

"Yes! She said, your little girl is really excelling. I told her, she must get all those crazy dance moves from Jenna." They laughed.

"You know I can *cut the rug* Austin!" She chuckled.

"Right. I'll talk to you later Jenna, we gotta get this plane ready for takeoff." He walked into the cockpit and took a seat. "I just briefed the relief crew."

"Ok. Me and Ron just did our walk around- didn't find anything- excellent plane."

"Great that's what I like to hear. Ron could you run those numbers again, and make sure we are good on weight." He reached over and grabbed the checklists, and Austin and Dan started running through them. They prepared the plane for taxi and made sure everything is set and ready to go. Then the passengers started to board. "Come on guys… come on out here and let's greet some passengers." One by one, passengers poured onto the plane. Austin, Dan and Ron greeted each one. "Hi." "Welcome aboard." "Hi how are you?" "Hey how're you doing?" Then, the suspicious man walked on board. He looked at Austin, coldly, held out his hand- without saying a word. Austin awkwardly shook the man's hand, and was just about to start a conversation, when the man turned and walked to his seat. Austin squinted and cut his eyes in confusion. This man was very peculiar in every way.

After about fifteen minutes, the flight attendants began the safety instructions. By now the plane was making its way onto the runway.

Austin got on the intercom and announced, "Alright ladies and gentlemen, this is the Captain speaking. We are number one for takeoff and will be in the air in just a few moments. Thank you all so much for choosing Dal Airlines, we should be in London in about twelve hours." Austin grabbed the throttle, and pushed it forward. Before you know it, the plane is soaring down the runway. Dan was calling out numbers and letters as the planes moved faster and faster, "90-100-V1-V2- rotate." At that moment Austin pulled the flight yoke backwards and the nose of the plane rose into the air. In a matter of seconds, the plane is flying. For a gentle second the plane felt weightless, perhaps why Austin always loved flying. He announced, "Gear up." Dan raises a lever and the tires fold up and store themselves into the plane.

When the plane was level, Jenna walked into the cockpit. "Hey guys what do you guys want to eat tonight- some chicken tetrazzini, or some roast beef?"

"I'll take the tetrazzini." Austin said.

"I'll take the roast beef!" Dan said.

"You just always have to do something different don't you?" Austin teased. Jenna laughed.

"Don't you talk to me about different Austin, you are *as crazy as it gets*, so you can't talk about anybody for being different." Dan chuckled.

"Ron what do you want?" Austin asked.

"Yeah Ron, you're the deciding factor in this, what do you want today?"

"Um, I think I want the roast beef." Ron said nervously.

"Aw Ron, you traded sides!" Austin said.

"I'm sorry sir, but you can never go wrong with some roast beef. Please don't be mad at me Captain…"

"Relax Ron. It was just a joke." Jenna turned and walked out. Austin reached up and turned the Fasten Seatbelt sign off. He grabbed the microphone and said, "Ladies and Gentlemen, you are now free to move about the cabin." He then looked over at Dan and Ron.

Suddenly a buzzer filled the cockpit. It sounded just like the buzzer in Austin's childhood dream. Austin began to zone out, only hearing the buzzer and not his crew. Dan reached over and turned a dial, and the buzzer went off. "Austin." A concerned Dan said. Austin blinked a few times, refocusing back to reality. He was still hearing the gun shots that murdered the boy outside of his window more than 30 years later. Austin blankly looked out of the cockpit windows.

"Uuuoh." Dan said to Ron, "He's got that look in his eye. What is it Austin?"

"Dan, I want to start a youth organization."

"What do you mean a *youth organization*?"

"I mean I want to start a youth organization. I do. I really do…"

"I don't know Austin I really don't."

"Why?"

"I just don't. I mean, look at us right now. We are at 39,000 feet…"

"…exactly and I want more young people to be able to experience this view. You don't know how many 'trouble youth' I grew up around. I mean, I grew up around a lot. And, they had *so* much potential Dan, they did, they had *so much potential*," He whispered, "But no one ever took the time to show them that they had it."

"You know Austin, just because something sounds good doesn't necessarily mean that it's a good idea. We have been best friends for years, and you know that I have your back, but I just don't think that it's a good idea."

"You know Dan, I was hoping that you would be a part of this."

"Austin, I don't even see how I *can* be a part of it! How do I have time for that? Think about it, most pilots aren't married anyway- the hours are too demanding- you are gone half of your family's life. How do you have time to start an organization and *now* you're going to be with *that* for who knows how long."

"Look, I never said that it was going to be easy. But I do think that it's doable…

"…it's not that it's not *doable* Austin, it's just that I just don't think that it's a good Idea…"

"…I don't see why- I want to be memorable, I want to be relevant. I forget what my director said, but it was something about if you're not relevant then people will simply forget about you. Right? And right now what makes us worthy of being in history books? I want to make a difference in someone's life. I want to change something."

"Austin, you're talkin' crazy. You know I love you, you're like a brother to me, but... what does your wife say?"

"She supports it."

"I mean, hey, if you guys are in then I'm in. We live the same life, but I just don't see how you have time to start an organization because I don't, and you have a family and I don't. So I just don't... whatever, I'm with you. Whatever."

At home, Ashley was doing laundry...

"Dang it Austin! This man here, he keeps leaving stuff in his pockets. Now the washer is all jammed up." Ashley pressed the start button over and over again. "Come on washer! Come on! Don't give out on me yet!" The washer spits and sputters and makes all kind of noises.

"What's wrong with the washer?" Mia asked. Suddenly, a tight shirted man walked in. "Um, excuse me, I think I may be able to help."

"Who are you!? Mia go upstairs baby!" Mia ran away. "Why are you in my house!?"

"I'm sorry, my name's Tyler." He walked very close to her. He stared at her in awe; he double talked and stuttered, and worked up enough courage to shake her hand. "Yeah, I was just coming by because they dropped off your package at my house, *and* to tell you that your garage door was open. You know… you have the most beautiful eyes that I've ever seen." She chuckled and blushed as he rubbed her cheek. "You know, I could probably fix that washer *no problem* for you."

"No I can just call the company to come fix it."

"*Shh*" he put his finger over her lips and began to talk really low. "If you call the company they are going to charge you hundreds of dollars. I'll do it for free."

"Oh yeah? And why would you do that?"

"Oh just to see you walk by me everyday baby. I'll go get my tools."

"I don't know about all of that, but if you can fix this washer for me, then do what you have to do. I'll just be in the kitchen making *my husband's* favorite meal."

"Oh so you're married? Where's your husband, I would like to meet him."

"He's on his way to London, on business; he's a pilot you know?"

"Oh, a pilot? What kind of man would leave you in this house all by yourself?"

"It's his job remember? So could you can just go get your tools please?"

"Ok, fine." He took off his shirt, he claimed it was a little warm, must've been the stove, or maybe Ashley. He walked back out of the house to his truck and Ashley watched, biting her lip- staring. "Oh shoot the food is burning!" Ashley quickly turned around and took the pan off the burner, then looked at the celling for a minute, not sure what to make of this Tyler guy.

Austin's journal:

I miss my wife, London's great, but I really miss my family. I told Dan about the organization that I'm trying to start. I really thought that he would be in; he says he's in, but I don't think he means it. I'm only writing these stupid journals because my wife thought it would be a good thing if our family wrote journals and share then with each other years later. Maybe this will make up for an anniversary or birthday or something that I forget. I met this little boy named River, I think that's my inspiration for Takeoff.

Ashley's Journal:

It was a rough day teaching dance. I'm trying to teach adults moves that kids get in seconds. One old lady, she's about 65, is trying to take my classes, did some move and sprung her hip or something like that. We had to call the paramedics and it was just a mess. The washer went out (I wonder if Austin is still writing these?) any way the washer went out today......... and this dude named Tyler came by to fix it. He says it won't be fixed for about a week, he's waiting on some parts or something like that. Tyler.... He's good with the kids, he took Jordan to the park to play basketball, and Mia, and she likes him. He's definitely a good role male figure while Austin isn't home. Hopefully he doesn't think that there is anything between us, because I'm happily married........ I think.

Chapter 3

After a fun-filled and eventful five days, the crew gathered early in London's flight crew relaxation room, all eager return home.

"Good morning Dan how ya' doing?" Dan glanced at him. "How'd ya' sleep? You look rough." Austin chuckled.

"Well, y'all had me out all night at the movies. That movie was awful! I'm trying to figure out who all of those actors were. That must've been one of those low budget movies."

"It better not have been, they charged us the full price." They laughed.

Austin noticed Dan's computer, "What are you doing?" He questioned.

Dan, full of delirium said, "I'm trying to check this weather; it was looking rough out there this morning."

"Yeah it was, but we should be fine, we've flown through worst." The 2nd officer cautiously walked up, "Hey Ron" Austin greeted the newcomer.

"Hey Captain. I just ran some of the numbers. Could you come look'em over?"

"Sure."

"Hey Austin, Hold on a minute, uh, you may want to see this." Austin turned to Dan, but Dan only pointed to the TV. The two stared at it, not sure what to say. The TV was mute, but they knew what the meteorologist was saying. She swayed back and forth- moving her hands in circle. Yes, the TV was mute, but she was talking up a storm.

"What? Oh shoot, severe thunderstorm warning. And it doesn't end until tomorrow. Dang that's a big storm."

"Are you telling me that we are stuck in London for another day?" Austin tapped on his phone, looking for evidence that the delay was an error. His screen read "INDEFINITELY."

"Hey Captain, um, it says the flight is delayed on the screens... what's going on?"

"It is. Indefinitely."

"What! Why?" Tamara said.

"Well, just hold on for one moment, I'm going to wait until everyone gets here." He said calmly.

John Paul entered the room and sashayed up to Austin. "Um, Austin, I mean Captain! It says that the flight is delayed? Why are we delayed Captain?"

"John Paul just wait til' everyone gets here."

"Hey Jenna, is everybody here? He asked, looking around her. "Where's Robinson, is she here yet?"

"Who?" Someone called out. "Me," Jackie replied as she wandered in. She gave Austin a glare.

Captain Austin just grinned but continued. "Ok everyone, it looks like the flight has been delayed indefinitely, perhaps even cancelled."

Austin paced back and forth, hands clasped nervously behind his back as the crew murmured about this negative turn of fortune. "From the news report, it looks like we are under a severe thunderstorm warning and the airport has been shut down. We are not going anywhere until it is lifted." He glanced at his watch. "And right now that could very well be tomorrow. It's a bad storm."

"So are we just supposed to stay in London another day?"

"It looks like Dal Airlines will be putting us up in hotel rooms for another day. So call your families, let them know that you didn't die in a plane accident or something, because that's the first thing that runs through my wife's mind if I'm even twenty minutes late. Speaking of, I better call her, and you guys call your families and let them know what's going on"

He took out his phone, and dialed home. "Hey Ash!"

"Hey Austin!"

"Did you sleep well last night?"

"I slept pretty well. How are you on the phone with me if your flight is supposed to leave soon?"

"It was supposed to, but there is a bad thunderstorm, and the flight is delayed and so we are stuck in London."

"Oh, well when do you think you'll be home?"

"Definitely tomorrow night, but right now this storm is really bad so we're stuck."

"Ok, well you be safe, and come home. I love you." Ashley said trying to keep from crying. Ashley suffered from separation anxiety, stemming from some childhood trauma. When Austin was away, she would pick up his picture every day and rub her fingers across his face.

"Love you too. Austin replied. Hey, you said the washer went out right? How's it coming? Because when I talked to you yesterday you said it still wasn't working right? And the *Tyler guy*, how's all of that coming?"

"Tyler is coming over every day to tinker with it, but he says he's waiting on a part."

"How much are we paying this guy?"

"Nothing, he said he'd do it for free."

"Why would he do it for free? It's like a $500 repair."

"I don't know. I- do- not- know." She said with regret in her voice. To Ashley, Austin was her polygraph. He always could tell when she was lying, so there was really no use in trying. She was falling for Tyler, at least while Austin was gone.

"Well alright, keep me posted, I'll talk to you and the kids later tonight. Love ya'. Bye."

Jenna completed her call as Austin was completing his. "So Austin, how's the kids?" "You know Jenna, the kids are doing great. How's your people?"

"They are doing alright. I have to pay the sitter extra to watch the little one overnight."

"Don't you hate that? Ashley had to go to a dance convention one time and my flight was late, so I was thirty minutes late to pick up Jordan, and it was $100 extra. Drives me crazy."

Jenna held up her index finger, "Oh wow, hold on Austin, let me call my mom."

"I need to call my partner, and let him know that I won't be home tonight. I know he's going to miss me." John Paul said, purposefully rubbing his relationship in everyone's face.

"Ok then John, let me call my dad." Austin stated. The phone rang, "Hey dad."

"Hey. How's London treating you?"

"It's nice; it's not as nice as maybe Paris, but nice. It looks like we'll be here a little bit longer though; thunderstorms."

"Ummhuum." Austin always loved when his father said that. He never knew what to think, did he dad *know*, or was just simply *agreeing*? Perhaps he didn't even believe him.

"So could you do me a favor and take Jordan fishing tomorrow?"

"Where at the park or something?"

"It doesn't matter, it's just that I promised him we would go fishing, but I won't be home until tomorrow night. Just teach him everything that you taught me." Austin's dad coughed with extreme intensity, it sounded like it hurt. "Dad are you ok?"

"Yep, I'm alright, just been coughin' real bad, but your mother's been taking care of me."

"Well, tell mom I said hi!"

"Alright, I'll talk to you later."

"Ok. Bye."

The next day Russ and Danielle, Austin's parents, drove over to Austin and Ashley's house to take the kids fishing. As soon as Russ' feet crossed the door's threshold, he was ready to go. He loved to fish, even thought about making it his career. "Jordan you ready to go!?" Russ said. "Where are we going grandpa?"

"We're going fishing son."

"Fishing? I'm supposed to go fishing with my daddy."

"Yeah, I know, but your mom told you that he won't be home until tonight right? So, I'm gonna take you fishing today."

"Jasmine, I mean Mia, You don't want to go?"

"NO! I'm going to my room. I'll be out when you can get my name right." Russ' memory had been fading on him lately. This bothered Austin; he couldn't stand the sight of his *ageing* father. Austin preferred to see his father the way he was when he was growing up, but that wasn't going to happen.

Mia was struggling with her father's *in and out lifestyle*, so everything was irritating to her.

"Alrighty then miss attitude. Ashley Who's this young man?"

"This is Tyler" Ashley said, "He's *trying* to fix the washer." Tyler glanced and smirked at her. Russ walked over to shake his hand, "I'm Russ Jackson, Austin Jackson's father. You know you're going to need a bigger wrench for that job son. I have one in the truck that will fit." Russ walked out to his truck, and Danielle headed up the stairs after Mia while Jordan went to get dressed. Tyler and Ashley were momentarily alone once more.

"What you mean tryin' to fix the washer baby?"

"I'm not your baby. And hush, my kids are upstairs. Besides, we're only having a little thing, don't make it emotional, because I am married. " She said poking his chest with her finger.

"Girl you know I want you." He winked and blew Ashley a kiss. Russ walked back in holding his wrench, "Here you go, this'll get it done." Jordan, fully dressed, ran down the stair and stood next to his grandpa.

"Alright Ashley we're out."

"Alright, Jordan be good with your Grandpa." She said.

Jordan Sighed, then put on his hat and yelled, "Ok. SHOTGUN!" Jordan bolted to the car.

"Ok, well I guess the boy ain't realized that my truck don't have a back seat anyway. See y'all later." The grandfather and grandson pair left.

The house was quiet. There was just the sound of the air conditioner blowing a plant on the kitchen table that Austin got Ashley for Valentine's Day. Tyler jingled and jangled his tools, while periodically winking at Ashley. Danielle had come down from talking with Mia, and sat at the kitchen table.

Ashley took a seat with Danielle. "So Ms. Danielle, can I get you some tea?"

"Naw suga, I'll just take some coffee." Danielle said.

"Sure."Ashley walked in the kitchen and pressed the power button on the coffee maker.

"So how have things been going lately?" Danielle asked.

"Things have been fine. Austin comes home today, I'm excited! The house is clean! So things are fine. Why do you ask?" Ashley gave her a cup of coffee. Danielle sipped and said, "Well, you just seemed like something was bothering you- that's all."

"Well…Ms. Danielle, your son is trying to start an organization."

"Really, that's good. He didn't tell me about that. You know Austin has always been what I call a go-getter. He's always been destined for greatness. He's always been different from everyone else, and that differentness is what I think makes him who he is. He's always been like that, since he was a baby, as a little kid, the other kids would play, and he would sit with me and *watch* the other kids play. So he's always been weird, but it always works out. When you think about it, some of the most successful people in the world are some of the craziest, and weirdest. So I knew that he would be something great. He taught me that being normal is 1) boring and 2) it's normal to be broke. It's normal to be middle class, and even though that's what he is now, I know that he's working to get out of it, because he's not normal, but extraordinary."

"Ms. Danielle I don't know what you're talking about…"

"I'm saying baby, that he will be successful in whatever he does. Have faith in your husband."

"So how far, do you think he's going to take this thing?"

"If I know my son correctly, he's going to take it all the way… what's he going to call it?"

"I don't know, I think he's going to call it Takeoff or something like that…"

"Oh ok, I kinda like that… Takeoff. And is it like a flight academy?"

"Something like that. But how far do you think that he will take this thing though?"

"I don't know. If I know my son, he's going to take it all of the way- as far as he can take it. And at the end of all of that pain, confusion, frustration, anger and crying, there will be success. That's what I *do* know, that he will not put his all into something, and it not be successful. I *will* tell you this though, it will not be easy- you're not always going to understand his plan. Sometimes he doesn't even have the words to vocalize his plan."

"I don't know Ms. Danielle, it's just hard to trust him and I don't even know *if he knows* what he's doing. He sold my car Ms. Danielle… and I've been trying to trust him, but sometimes, I feel like I don't even know who he is… "

"…trust your husband. It'll all work out. Trust him." The ladies chatted and sipped their coffees; Danielle trying to help Ashley deal with her changing emotion towards Austin. They talk for hours about Ashley's feelings and needs when suddenly a car slams on breaks in front of their house, visible through the big kitchen window. Two guys took out guns and each took a shot at the house. "POW. POW." Ashley and Danielle fell to the floor, breaking their coffee cups. Tyler already on the floor yells, "Stay down!" One of the guys shot one more time. "Let's go! GO! GO! GO!" The shooters yelled speeding away. The shots finally stopped. For a moment those seconds of gunfire turned into hours. There was a silence. The only sound was the uneasy silence that covered the house. No one said anything.

Tyler stood up, looking at the kitchen window, "What was that? Nothing like that has ever happened in this neighborhood before!"

Ashley stood up shaking off her clothes, "Is everyone ok? Yes?" She glanced over where the shooting took place. "My window, they shot through the window!"

Danielle rolled over, then stood up saying, "Let me go check on Mia."

"Oh yes, my baby girl!" Ashley announced.

"Don't worry I'll check on her." Danielle reassured.

"Tyler look at this window! And look at what they did to my wall- Tyler what am I going to do?" Ashley's mind began to race. She could only imagine what Austin would do if he found out that there house was the target of a drive-by shooting.

Tyler walked up to Ashley and grabbed her hands, "Listen…Hey look at me… we can fix this. I have a friend who does construction, he can get me a window in a matter of minutes, and I'll fix the holes in the wall, everything's gonna be ok…"

"What about when Austin finds out? He's gonna want to move! I love this house I can't move."

"That's true, you can't. So here's what we'll do, we just won't tell him. I'll go call my friend and have him bring that window and I'll work on these walls, but look, no police though. It'll just make things worse."

"Thanks Tyler." Ashley smiled.

"Aww baby that's what I live for- to see that smile of yours."

"Stop it Tyler. Our little thing has to stop…"

"…I thought that there wasn't a thing…"

"…Oh you know what I'm talking about…"

At the park, Russ and Jordan were having a much better time…

"Jordan, you see this worm right? Ok we are going to put him on this hook. We are going to take him…. And slide…..him….. Up like this……. And a little more, and boom he's on there."

"Why is he moving around like that?" Jordan asked.

"It's kind of like getting a shot; you know how when you get a shot you move a little bit? That's how it is."

"Grandpa? Can I ask you a question?"

"Of Course."

"Grandpa, does my daddy love me?"

"What do you mean Jordan, of course he does, why would you even ask something like that?"

"Mia says that sometimes daddies leave and go with other families and stuff like that. And that's why he's never home with us."

"Now listen to me! Your father loves you more than life itself! Don't listen to that stuff your sister is telling you! I'm telling you that it's not true. And you knew that already, you know that he loves you! So don't ever question that again. Looks like I will need to have talk with him.

Now just press the button like that… and cast it back like this… there you go! Now we wait."

Mia's Diary:

You know, my mom really likes Tyler. Or at least that how it seems. I like him too. He's nice, and kind. He takes care of me and my brother. He taught Jordan basketball tricks, my brother sucks at it so… That's stuff my dad should be doing, but he's not here, so maybe that's why my mom like Tyler. I don't know. I just know that whatever is going on, it's not right.   And the shots fired today? What was that about? My mom said she didn't want me to tell my dad, like I would ever… I don't know what the big deal is though- she made it into a big deal- yelling at me and stuff, "DON'T TELL YOUR FATHER!!" she said. I was like……whaaaatevveerr

Jordan's Journal

Mia said that some body shot at the house. I didn't know what to do, and my dad said to look after every body. So I called him. He told me I did a good job for calling him, but he was kinda upset too, he was talking to himself about how he would use that against mommy one day. Whatever that means, oh well daddy will handle it. He's like superman.

Chapter 4

Today the sun shined bright in London. The roar of jet engines ran through the airport, that sound could instantly recharge Austin, as he sat in the Captain's chair.

"Alright Dan it's a new day! The storms are moving out of here, and I'm ready to get home! So let's get out of here." Austin grabbed the microphone and said, "Flight attendants please begin cross check and all call." It was important for the flight attendants to do that-they made sure that the doors were closed and secure. Austin then looked at Dan, "It's time to go Dan! I'm excited." Ron looked up, sitting behind the two pilots.

"We'll talk a little bit more on that little idea of yours- the organization. I haven't forgot about it."

"Well, I was hoping that you wouldn't forget about it, and that your position on it would change."

"Well, you know how that goes." Dan said looking off.

"Ron what do you think?" Austin asked.

"Excuse me sir?"

"What do *you* think of me starting a nonprofit organization?"

"Well, I'm going to be honest with you Captain…"

"…Oh boy…" Austin mumbled.

"See, I told you. Ron's on my side." Dan said gladly.

"…Captain, I really wish that I had something like that when I was growing up. It really would've made this process a lot easier, but sir I will tell you, it won't be easy. As the first officer stated, it will be very difficult- we do live very busy lives, and to do that and basically run a company… because starting an organization is just like starting a company, so I just know that it won't be easy to do sir."

"You know what, thank you for that." Austin smirked at Dan, "See, someone believes in me."

"Yes sir I do." Ron said.

The flight took off. The crew was pretty quiet that day. There was a knock at the cockpit door. After checking the peep hole, Austin answered it. "Ah our relief." He announced. He got up and let the relief pilot take over saying, "Good night you guys. I'm gonna go and take me a quick nap." He turned and walked out of the cockpit. Once out, his eyes met with the same man from the coming flight. Austin looked at him, while the man stared back, still dressed in black. Austin greeted the man, and continued his walk down the aisle. 8 hours later, Austin, Dan and Ron were well rested and took the controls from the relief crew.

The flight landed back in Atlanta, Georgia. The crew was over the moon to be back home with their families. The Captain announced on the intercom, "Ladies and Gentlemen, on behalf of the entire flight crew here at Dal Airlines, I would like to welcome you to Atlanta Georgia, local time is 6:42 pm." One by one, starting with the peculiar man dressed in black, the passengers left the plane. After the last one left, Austin announced, "Alright guys I'm gone." He was glad to almost be home with his family and his kids, especially after his dad told him what Jordan said. "See ya' Jenna, see ya' Ron." "Ok see you." they replied.

Austin took a taxi home from the airport. Pulling up to his house, he saw a shirtless man. "Hey! Uh, who are you?" Austin asked in panic.

"I'm Tyler." The man replied, "Who are you?"

"Well, this is my house, so you don't really get to ask that question."

"Oh, you must be Austin. Hey man, I'm fixing the washer for your wife? Did she mention me?"

"Oh yes, that's right. She did. How ya' doing Tyler? I just got back from London, and I'm tired, so let me go see the family, we'll talk later."

"Alright then." Tyler walked to his truck. Austin walked inside of his house. Little footsteps ran towards him. "DADDY!" Jordan yelled. "Come on Mia, Dad's home!"

"Hey Jordan!" Austin said, looking around for damage, but there was none. Since there was no damage, he wasn't even going to bring it up to Ashley, he assumed it must've been one of Jordan's little dreams. "What's up buddy?" He asked. "You know what, I heard that you did really well fishing yesterday?"

"I did, I wish that you would've been there…"

"Me too buddy, me too, but you know, it was a bad storm in London so they wouldn't let us leave."

"They were keeping you there?"

"Yep, the storm was that bad. So we had to stay in London."

"How long are you home this time?"

"I'll be home for the next two weeks. Y'all will be sick of me soon." He chuckled.

"Yay. *Dad's* home." Mia said sarcastically, arms crossed and rolling her eyes.

"Mia come here. Look, now, I don't know what wrong with you, but I want you to know that I love you. I do. I really do. There's people that don't have fathers you know?"

"Well, to be honest dad, I kinda feel like I'm one of them." She turned around and walked away. Austin stood there and stared, shocked by her words.

"Hey Ash!"

"Hey Baby!" Ashley ran to Austin and jumped into his arms. "I missed you."

"I know I missed you too. Even though we've been talking every day, I still missed waking up next to you." Tyler was staring in the background. They walked towards the kitchen. "Hey Ms. Margaret, how are you? I didn't know your mom was here Ashley."

"Fine honey, but I'm hungry I'm going to get something to eat." Margaret walked to the kitchen. Austin and Ashley followed.

"Mom, we have food in there you know?" Ashley said.

"I know, where did you think I was getting something to eat from?" Austin put his bag in a kitchen chair.

"Ok....Alrighty...well... good to be home."

"Well, Captain Austin, How was London?" Margaret asked.

"London was ok, it was nice, it just wasn't as good as maybe Paris or somewhere like that. It was very old…"

"OH MY GOSH! OH MY GOSH OH MY GOSH!" Ashley's sister exclaimed running into the kitchen

"Hey!" Ashley responded with excitement. Perhaps she thought it was a shoe sale or something?

"What are you doing here exactly?"

"I have a major announcement!"

"Girl what is it?" Ashley asked.

"Look at this, BAM!" she pulls her hand out of her pocket and shows them a ring on her finger.

"Oh ok, you've been to the 99 cent store again haven't you?"

"WHAT! NO ASHLEY! This is my engagement ring." Ashley's face froze between embarrassment and humiliation.

"Oh. Ok great! I'm so excited for you, now you gotta tell me, who's the lucky guy?"

Tyler walked in and crept up behind Regina. He rapped his hands around her waist.

"Hey baby." He said.

"His name is Tyler." Regina announced.

"Oh. Um, Tyyyllleeerr... ok." Ashley says awkwardly. "Oh, well who knew? I definitely didn't know that you guys were an item." She continues more awkwardly. So many thoughts ran through Ashley's mind. *'Why was he all flirty? Is this a joke?'* She knew more than anything that she has to keep herself together.

"Well I'm just happy you're marrying somebody. He must have money?" Margaret proclaimed. "Naw, never mind, he can't have *that much* or he wouldn't have bought you that little bitty thing on your finger."

"Momma!" said Regina.

"What? That girl thought it was a dollar store ring! That should tell you something right there! IT'S SMALL!"

"Tyler, you didn't tell me that you knew my sister." Ashley persisted.

"Yeah, well, I do, and she's my fiancée." He said kissing Regina's neck.

"AAHHHAA! Who knew? Right babe?" Austin said in genuine surprise. His original worry about Tyler disappeared, realizing he was in love his sister in law and not his wife.

"Ummhuuum. Right. Well, Austin can I talk to you in the den?"

"Sure." They walk to the next room over clumsily bumping into the corner of the couch- their footsteps were anxious, and deceivingly calm.

"Ok, so while you were gone- now hear me out before you fly off the handle- while you were gone the washer broke Tyler came by to fix it and all of that. So the entire time he's been here, he's been hitting on me…"

"… and you let him stay and keep coming back?"

"Well I do need the washer fixed, and he offered for free. And just because he throws around some compliments with a smile doesn't mean I'm just going to drop my clothes…"

"... I would definitely hope not! You *are* my wife..."

"... I know baby, but now what are we going to do?"

"So what you're saying is that he likes you, but he's marrying your sister? Maybe tell her?"

"Ok, but only after the washer is fixed." They laughed.

"Ok, but now we have to walk out of here and pretend that we were talking about something else." They walk out of the den laughing and smiling, "Don't you just hate when that happens Ash?"

"When what happens?" Tyler asked.

"Um, when people put lipstick on their teeth. It's a pet peeve of mine." They chuckle. Austin and Ashley periodically glanced at each other, thinking the same thing, at the same time. They had a really crazy connection, but it was what made them unique.

Ashley's Diary :

OH LORD SOMEBODY HELP ME! My sister's fiancé has a thing for me! I need some help Jesus. This is the kind-of- thing that happens in those movies, but you never think that it really will happen to you... well me. I don't know what I'm going to do. The sad part about it though, is that I kinda like it. Does that make me a bad person? But no I don't like it because I'm married, but I do like it, he's a very nice guy, but I......... I...... I'm going to stop writing now, before I mess myself up.

Chapter 5

"Come on kids lets go fishing" Austin said.

Jordan hugged his father and said, "Yay we get to go fishing again! Come on Mia!"

"I don't want to go fishing." Mia said. She crossed her arms and rolled her neck.

"Come on Mia, Let's go."

"I don't want to go." She rolled her neck again.

"Well, we'll be in the car waiting on you." said Austin.

"Mom! I don't want to go!"

"Mia! Listen to your father. Go on honey."

"Fine." She said. They got in the car and drove away. The ride was silent. Jordan stared out of the window and Mia sat in the back seat, arms folded and pouting. Pulling up to the park Mia said, "This place looks old."

"Yeah dad where are we?"

"This is an old lake, it's an old park that I actually use to come to when I was about your age Mia. We used to fish and fish and fish, never thought that there were any real fish in here though. My dad always claimed it was big fish in here. He would always say, 'oh yeah son, I caught a big one today' but for some reason never managed to bring them home. So before we get started, there's something I need to talk to you guys about. I wanted to talk about what *you* told your grandfather, and what *you* have been telling your brother. I do not have another family first of all…"

"Then why are you always gone?"

"I'm a pilot Mia, it's what I do. I travel the world, taking people from place to place. I go somewhere, I stay there for four days, then I'm home for another five. That's just how my schedule works. I'm gone, I'm back, I'm gone I'm back. So I don't know what to tell you. I really don't. You are the only family that I want. You two, and your mom, are the only family that I have, that I need."

"Are you sure?"

"I'm pretty sure Mia. You're the only family that I have. If I don't have my family, then I have nothing. You all are the only family that I have- you, your brother, your grandmas and your grandpa. When you see me on video chat, and I'm in those fancy hotel rooms, it's because that's where the airline pays for me to stay. Because I'm staying in a nice hotel, doesn't mean that I'm meeting someone there, ok Mia, you need to stop watching some of those TV shows. As a kid, my director used to say that, they call it Television because it's *telling* you a *vision* that it wants you to see. Alright, you need to stop watching some of those reality shows, because they are messing with your mind, ok?"

"Ok." She shrugged her shoulders.

"I mean Jordan he's only six, he basically going to believe what his big sister is telling him. And you're telling him lies about me."

"I'm sorry dad." Mia looked up at him with tears in her eyes. That was the first time she looked him in the eyes. She began to cry.

"It's alright." He grabbed her and held her in his arms. "It's ok, it's alright baby girl. You're still my baby girl- the only daughter I have." He reached over and grabbed his son and brought him to the hug. "You too, little J, you're the only son I have. And I love you guys. So let's do some fishing." Austin stood up to get the fishing poles. "Oh yes, and I don't want you to ever say those lies again, ok." The children nodded. "Alright Jordan so this is what you are going to do, you see this worm?"

"It's nasty!" Mia said.

"Just watch closely, we're going to bait a hook. Alright, watch…"

Jordan interrupted "…dad, I already know how to do it."

"What?"

"Granddad showed me how to do it."

"Oh, ok then." Austin was a little disappointed that he didn't get to show Jordan *first*, how to fish. He did tell his dad to take him, but he still would have liked to show him how to do it first. "Ok, I'll just show you Mia. You're just going to take the hook, and run it up through him like this…"

"*Eeww* dad, why is he squirming around like that?"

"Oh I know, it's like when you get a shot." Jordan announced. Austin smirked in confusion. "A shot Jordan?"

"Yes, grandpa told me that it's like when you get a shot, and how you squirm when they stick you with the needle."

"Oh! Ok, I get it." Mia claimed.

"That makes since to you Mia?" Austin asked,

"Yes. I get it now."

"Ok? It's like getting a shot." Austin said. "So now that he's on there, you're going to press and hold the button, and put it over your shoulder- look behind you, then throw the pole forward like that."

"Daddy, can I show her?" Jordan begged. Austin's Phone rang.

"Sure Jordan. I'll be right over here ok?" He answers his phone, "Hello? Hey, yes this is Austin. *Umhum*, really? How much is it? Oh! Ok, alight well, I'm going to have to talk to my wife about it. Send me an e-mail with all of that information on there, and we'll come by tomorrow and talk to you about it."

"Daddy do you see me?" Jordan yelled.

"I see you buddy! Ok talk to you later then, just send me that e-mail and we should be by sometime tomorrow. Alright, bye." He put the phone back in his pocket. "I see you Mia, you're getting the hang of it, oh, remember to look behind you. Now what if I was standing there, you would've hooked me." They laughed. Austin took his phone back out, and called Ashley. "Hey Ash, the realtor just called me, he is trying to get us a building."

"A building for what babe?"

"For Takeoff."

"Wait, what? You're looking for a building for that?"

"I mean, yeah, what was I going to do our sessions or trainings in- the garage?"

She chuckled, "I just didn't think that... that you would... can I ask you a question?"

"Sure."

"What's your plan? Like, what are you trying to do?"

"Well, you already know that I'm trying to make a difference..."

"…yes but how do you want to go about this business part of it? Buying building and flyers, and pamphlets and stuff like that."

"Right now, I've just been doing them myself, and trying to make things happen. You know I'm trying to change some people's lives…"

"Well, listen, I want to be there for you- *not half be there*, but you have to let be there. Ok? I want know everything with the business, I want to be a part of it."

"Of course babe, my friend just called and there's a place that we can get. It's supposed to be nice- it's ok though, it's a little old, and a little raggedy, but with a little TLC, it should be a nice building. You want to go see it with me tomorrow?"

"I would like that."

"So would I."

"You know babe, I really do support this. I really do." Ashley said.

"I know, it's just- I have a problem letting people be there for me- I'm working on it, it's just after so many people let you down, you kind of stop working with anybody. But like I said, I'm working on that, that's my own issue. It's just that sometimes when so many people don't support you, it's hard to recognize the people that do."

"Well you better recognize, fast." They both laughed. "Come on home though, we need some *us* time."

"I'm on the way. Bye. Kids let's go!" As Austin turned around, the man dressed in black was sitting in a car- staring. Austin waved at the man, hoping these encounters were just a cluster of strange coincidences, but the man sped off.

Austin's Journal:

You know it's very refreshing to actually have someone believe in me. Everyone around me doesn't think it's a good idea. They think it's a stupid idea, and then there's my wonderful wife, who is driven and optimistic about the future. I'll give it to her, I thought these journals were a pretty stupid idea, but I'll give it to her, they do help— a lot. I straightened things out with my kids, so it should be smooth sailing from here on out. Takeoff will soon be airborne. That sounds kinda lame, I'm gonna brainstorm on some catch phrases.

_____

_____

_____

Mia's diary

I can't believe it! Today was the best day of my life! My DADDY LOVES ME. He told me that we were the only family for him, and he just loves me!!! I'm so excited. I was wrong about him! He really loves me! But what about mom, Aunty Regina and Mr. Tyler? I may be young, but I know that something weird is going on there.

Chapter 6

It was an amazing day today. Lately in Atlanta, The days have been sunny, and the temperature and the breeze just right. Simply put, the days have been perfect. Austin and Ashley drove to the realty office to meet with their realtor, a man named Baz. After seeing the building they intended to use for Takeoff, Austin asked, "So Baz how much is this building going to cost?"

"Well it will only cost 500,000, but I promise you it's a bargain." Baz pointed at a contract.

"WOH, That's a lot of Zeros there Baz."

"Babe, can we afford that?" Ashley asked.

"We should be able to afford it, but I mean, *woo*, that's a lot of Zeros. Ashley can you give us a minute?"

"What? Why?" she questioned.

"Just give me a minute, come on baby." Ashley rolled her eyes, and reluctantly walked out to the car.

Baz continued, "It's costly, but you have to look at what you're getting. You're getting an office that will bring in revenue, so I think it's worth it."

"Well Baz this is for a nonprofit organization that I'm starting called Takeoff."

"Oh. Well that's ok; this is still a nice building. I know it's a little older, but to me that says charm, and I think that that will definitely help lure people into Takeoff." Baz was quite the fast talker. He could sell you something before you realize you wanted it. He even sold Austin their house, and they were only 'just looking.'

Austin really wanted to get the building, but there was a strange ringing in the back of his head-

Ashley. He feared what she would have to say. He knew that she *said* she was supportive of Takeoff, but didn't quite know how far that support would last. "Closing costs are included, and so, when you sign this contact, and put some money down, then you are good to go. I can get you the keys *today*!"

Suddenly Austin blacks out-staring at the paper and pen in hand. He was seeing something, what some might call a vision. In the vision there was a knock at Baz's door. Baz opened the door and Austin saw screaming children. "PLEASE HELP ME!" "CAN YOU HELP ME? PLEASE?" The children cried. They were begging for a chance in the world. A chance to be something. Perhaps the first one in their family to go to college, or the first one to be a success. They were morphing in front of Austin. The kids morphed into adults-faces blurred. They appeared to be homeless- holes in their clothes, scruffy and rough looking, barely any teeth in their mouths, very skinny, starving. These once were the children crying out to Austin, and he was powerless. He said to himself, "Antonio? Kathy?" He then saw a kid. He looked six years old or so. The boy was being gunned down by some street thugs. The boy yelled through the door, "AUSTIN HELP! PLEASE HELP" The door slammed shut, a gunshot and a gush of air followed.

"Austin?" Baz said nudging him. He looked up at him, grasping reality, "Do you think I should do it?" Austin asks Baz.

"I really do." Austin took the pen and rereads the contract. He nervously looked around, and signed on the dotted line. Austin grabs the keys from Baz and after filling out some paper work, walks outside with Ashley. He got in the car, and looked at Ashley for a minute or two- gathering his thoughts. He was trying to be tactful in telling Ashley what he had just done.

"Ash?" She looked at him. He reached in his pocket and pulled out the new gold keys, "We're owners now."

"Wait? You did what now?"

"I got the place. I got a deal on it…"

"..Austin 500,000 dollars isn't a deal. I can't believe you did this? What are we gonna do?

"We're gonna have to move." Austin put the car in drive, and drove away- confident that Ashley took it better than he thought, and sure that she was truly supporting him.

"I'm sorry? What do you mean we're gonna have to move?

"We're going to have to stay at an apartment. I have a friend that can get us a great deal!"

"What! Why?"

"Ash, you know we can't afford that place we just bought. I mean, we can afford it, but we can't afford it and stay where we are staying."

"Austin we are not living in luxury. We are living in a regular house, driving regular used cars, so it's not like we are living a fancy life or anything like that- and you're making a good bit of money."

"You're right babe, but this organization… it's gonna cost a lot- a whole lot."

"I mean I told you, my company is going to sponsor you, so you don't have anything to worry about. Just relax, we don't have to move or do anything drastic."

"No Ashley, we are going to have to move; I have to sell the house. We are going to need that money- soon."

"What? We aren't moving. *I'm not moving.*"

"Yes… Yes you are babe. Now look, I know that it's a little frustrating, and I know that it's a little different, but we are going to have to leave."

"No. I'm not going anywhere! And you're not taking the kids anywhere! We are not leaving *our house* to go live in an apartment because you decide to have an organization- that doesn't even make sense."

"Yes it does, we have to save money. Right? So that we can start this organization…"

"… So you're going to put this organization on the forefront and put your family on the backburner? But you can buy the nicest most exclusive facility for this organization. Really?"

"Now you know that that place is a pig-sty. You're just being dramatic, so don't sit here and pretend that it's so nice and that I spend money on it but not my family because that's a lie. Now you know, that to get this organization on its feet, it's gonna take a lot of money, and time, and our first session is this Saturday."

"Why didn't we just lease a place or something like that? I mean baby, that doesn't even make sense! And we just bought a building and you already had sessions lined up? Did you think that you were going to have our house sold by this Saturday?"

"No, but I do think that when we do sell our house, that that money would go towards this organization."

"So you are going to sell…our families living… for your organization's benefit? Is that what we're doing here?"

"That's right."

"YOU HAVE LOST YOUR MIND! I mean seriously you have lost your natural mind!"

"What are you talking about I haven't lost anything…"

"…pull this car over"

"We are going home so we can pack."

"PULL THIS CAR OVER NOW! Austin I'm not playing, pull this car over!" He pulls to the shoulder of the road. "What? What is it Ash?"

"Look, now I support your organization…"

"NO YOU OBVIOUSLY DON'T! If you did you would be willing to help anyway you can!"

"It's not about me wanting to help you!" she yelled, "YOU KNOW I WANT TO HELP YOU MORE

THAN ANYBODY ELSE, AND IF NOBODY ELSE SEES YOUR DREAM I DO, AND YOU KNOW THAT! BUT IT DOESN'T SEEM THAT YOU WANT TO HELP YOURSELF- YOU'RE NOT THINKING REASONABLY!"

"You're right I'm not, and guess what sugar plum, neither are they- the people out there that need our help. And you know it! I grew up with people who were raising their siblings. They were teenagers, playing mommy and daddy for their siblings. While their parents are out doing who knows what with who knows who. And you're asking them to be productive citizens. You're asking them to make honor roll when they have to help their siblings do homework and projects all night! Is that rational? Is that reasonable? Is it reasonable for some of the people that I know to be in gangs? Some of my good friends, turn around and join a gang, is that reasonable? The last thing that they are thinking about is their future. I've already lost about six friends over the years to simple ignorance! They weren't being reasonable! And perhaps if I would have told them some of the things I know about success and living your dreams that they would be alive today, and maybe they would have been a little more reasonable. YOU KNOW WHAT, SIT BACK WE ARE GOING TO TAKE A TRIP, LET'S GO DOWNTOWN! I can take you down there. And show you what will happen if I don't start this organization."

"Don't you move this car! We are talking. We are not about to argue and drive."

"Oh, so now you don't want to take a trip. Come on lets go downtown! Because guess what if we walk the streets I bet I know a good bit of the people down there holding up signs and sleeping under bridges. I've been down there and every time I go I double take at about half of the people, some of them look very different, some of them look the same way they did in school, just a little dustier. The people up under the bridges, the people on the highway's holding up signs *guess what*, they were in school with you one day. If I call out some names… I know for a fact my old friend Antonio is down there! But I have an opportunity now- I have an opportunity to give back, to help make some of these young people realize how much greatness they have in them. Maybe they will tell their friends, you just never know this could be a chain reaction- an *uproar* of success. Maybe because of my efforts our children's generation will be the most successful in history." Austin's eyes began to water. This was his passion "You know my story Ashley. You know I didn't have much. You know that I watched that little boy get shot. Right outside my window too- do you know how hard that is? To be that defenseless and that helpless? I did nothing!"

"Austin you were, what five? Eight?"

"I WAS SIX ASH. And was able to do nothing. I can't let that happen again. More and more young men are being killed for no reason, and young women- they don't know how valuable they are that they settle for anything and end up doing anything to fill valued. I mean come on Ash, you know how you were when we first met… you got with any and everybody. You were wild!"

"It was college."

"Yeah, and it almost killed you. Until you got yourself together and became a success. That's all I'm trying to do is help make other people as successful as we are, but you don't want to support that!"

"No, I want to support that and you know I do, so don't you even try and pull that on me! I SUPPORT YOU WHEN EVERYONE ELSE DOESN'T! WHEN EVERYONE ELSE GIVES UP ON YOU, AND YOU KNOW IT! But I don't want to support your foolishness! YOU WANT OUR FAMILY TO LEAVE OUR COMFORT, SO THAT YOU CAN USE THAT MONEY TO MAKE OTHER PEOPLE COMFORTABLE."

"Let me tell you something about selfless service…"

"… Don't you tell me nothing about selfless service I know about selfless service…"

"…let me finish! Sometimes you have to do something for someone else besides yourself! I became a pilot. I'm living the dream, now I need to give back and help someone else."

"It's not about helping someone else, but you want me to discomfort my own family… you want me to make our family homeless. That's what you want me to do! You're asking us to sell our house, and be homeless, and make room for other people's children? That's what you're saying?"

"And what's wrong with that? WHAT'S WRONG WITH ME WANTING OUR FAMILY TO LEARN THE VALUE OF HELPING OTHER PEOPLE?"

"Listen there is nothing wrong with helping other people, but you ain't even helped yourself. You haven't helped *this* family! You're trying to put our family out on the streets while you are running around being Jesus!"

"Listen baby, let me make this real clear, I'm going to do this, and it's just… that… simple."

"Well then you're going to do it by yourself, you are not selling my house!"

"Am I or am I not the head of this household? When we stood at the altar and said our wedding vows, you said that you would let me be the head of this household, now you let me be… the head… of my household."

"You can be the head of whatever you wana to be, you can be the head of your organization, you can be the head of our household, but what you won't be doing is selling our household, because then you will have nothing to be the head of."

"Fine. Fine."

"What do you mean by fine?"

"Fine." He drove home silent. The car had a strange and bitter quietness. The only sound that could be heard was the air conditioner. The silence was a mean silence, painful even. They walked into the house. "Hey dad!"

"Hey Mia. Did you have a good day today?"

"Yes, this girl was talking about me, and I took your advice, and I'm not going to let anybody worry me, because what she thinks of me doesn't matter right dad?"

"Right Mia. I like the way you said that."

"Mia could you take your brother and go upstairs?" Ashley asked.

"Ok, I'll talk to you later Mia." Austin said. The kids went upstairs. "You know Austin, you haven't said a word this entire time."

"Neither have you." he sharply replied.

"Ok. That was mature, *my husband*."

"My wonderful wife, I have to do this. I've got too."

"What makes you think that you are going to be the person to change these people's lives? I mean really, I'm being real, if they want to be homeless that's a choice. They choose that. It's a choice! There are options out there. If you don't take the options that are presented to you, then that's their fault. Why are you going to put this family in some way, because of their decisions?"

"Let me tell you something baby… you have your bags packed tomorrow morning, and if you think that you're staying here… it must be with the new buyers?"

Austin walked upstairs and read his son a bed time story. Then spent the rest of the night talking to his daughter about the mean girls in her class. Ashley didn't say one word to her husband that night.

The next morning, Ashley had her bags at the front door. Early that morning, Austin ran out and got some boxes for all of their things. Ashley didn't sleep well. She had been up all night packing. Jordan and Austin brought down 35 boxes one by one- all full of priceless memories and collections. The furniture was to stay in the house; their new apartment was fully furnished. Austin walked out of the house for a final time, as he crossed the door's threshold; he glanced over his shoulder at Ashley. She was looking from left to right at their now old house, sighing. The Jackson's and their movers arrived at their new apartment. Together they carried all 35 boxes in to the one bed room apartment. The apartment appeared to be new. Everything smelled fresh and off of the show room.

"Kids that's your room back there? Ashley me and you have the let out couch." Ashley glanced at Austin in Anger, then quickly glanced away realizing that the kids were watching. "It's not bad huh Ash?"

"It's alright."

"Ashley… you know that's the first word you've said in long time."

"Mia, go show your brother y'all's room." The children walked into the next room. "Austin honestly, I really can't believe I'm still with you."

"Ashley! How could you say that?"

"I'm just telling you how I feel right now. I've been doing some thinking, and seriously, I don't know why I'm still here."

"Ash…"

"… No I'm serious, I mean really, you sold my car, now my house, and you still haven't told me anything about this Takeoff mess."

"Don't call it mess Ash."

"I mean, hey, that's how I'm feeling right now."

"Ashley I really wish you could see what I see." Austin smiled.

"I wish I could too. And you know what, that's really getting to me too- why haven't you even tried to clearly explain this organization of yours, because at this point, this is sounding real stupid. And you know what; I'm the idiot for actually leaving my house to move into this one bedroom, for a stupid piece of sh…"

"…Ash…" he interrupted.

"…I'm sorry but I really am hurt. Please don't talk to me right now, just don't talk to me, I'm really in my feelings right now."

"Ashley you know, I learned some time ago that at the end of your feelings is nothing, but at the end of pain is success."

"Austin shut up with all those riddles and stuff. I mean seriously you have my family in this little old apartment, but it's really a waste of time because I'm going to let you know now, if this Takeoff mess doesn't takeoff, I will." Ashley assured avoiding eye contact.

Austin reached into one of the boxes and pulled out his cross that hung over the door at their old house. He found a nail lying on the freshly built fireplace and forced it into the wall. He hung the cross directly over the fireplace. He tapped the cross, "Ashley it'll all work out. Just trust your husband."

"Well it better or I'm gone!"

"Is that a threat?"

"Naw baby, it's a promise! I'm out of here if I don't start seeing something with this stupid Takeoff group soon!"

"Are you really that selfish? Wow you never know who you marry till you go through something."

"Yep, you're dang right. I feel the *exact, same, way.*

"You know what, I have work to do."

"I'm gonna leave. I'm gonna take my things and I'm going to leave."

"Why? Why are you leaving? You're always gone anyway why are leaving us like this? You brought us here and now you're leaving."

He whispered, "I have work to be done. I left my family in a good position. Cable TV, new everything, you're set. I have a session Saturday........ And I expect for *my wife* to be there. I expect *my children* to be there. Don't you want to be relevant? Don't you want to be remembered for something other than owning a dance company? You own a dance company. Congratulations, but whose life did you change? If you're not making someone else's life better than your wasting your time."

"Wasting my time? I help people change every day! Why do you think they come to have dance lessons? So they can learn something new and change themselves!" Listen baby, I think that you are doing a very noble, even an honorable thing by helping other people realize their potential, but you are taking it too far. You sold the house… so that you can have money for this organization."

"Baby, you have to look past what you see today. I was listening to this guy on the radio; I forget his name, Eric Thomas I think. He said that 'you are trying to live in the present and the future and you have to live in the forward' so don't get caught up in what you are seeing now."

"All of that is great, but it doesn't change the fact that you want to sell this house for somebody else."

"It's ok, because I'm just going to go and work. I want you to support my dream, how wrong am I? I get it, it's kind of hard to see right now, I get it, its ok." He grabbed his things and he walked towards the door.

"NO YOU DON'T GET IT AUSTIN YOU DON'T GET IT!"

"What part of this am I missing?"

"I can't handle another man leaving me."

"Oh but you can sure leave a man?"

"Please don't go. Come on baby don't leave. Don't leave me."

"Baby I'm not leaving you."

"You are, you have your suitcase packed, and you're leaving."

"I'm not leaving, I'm just going way for a few days to work on this organization."

"Listen you can call it whatever you want to try and call it. You can give it whatever kind of euphemism you want to, but you're leaving." She started crying.

"Oh no, don't cry."

"I'm not crying because I don't see what you see, I want you to know that. I will support you in your many different projects because I love you. I'm crying because I can't handle another person leaving me. My father left."

"I know he died."

"No, he left me and my mom when I was a child. He came back into my life just before we got married, and I'm still daddy's little girl so I accepted him. Honestly, Austin, let's just be real for a second, I honestly don't think I can survive another man walking out on me. I don't know what I'll do."

Austin grabbed her, and looked deep in her eyes, "Can you support my decisions for the better of Takeoff?" there was a silence. They both stared at each other. Tears filled both of their eyes. Austin wiped his face. "That's what I thought." He turned around and walked out of the door, carrying his boxes. Austin got in the car. Ashley stared at him through the window in disbelief. She was in shock. He drove off, and Ashley fell to her knees.

Jordan's Journal:

<u>Mommy and daddy are fighting again. My sister is gonea be mad when she finds out. But it will work out…. Right?</u>

Chapter 7

For the past few days, Austin has been away from his family staying at an old and decrepit hotel. Since he decided to launch Takeoff, he hasn't been able to think clearly, and his priorities are constantly shifting. He recently realized that moving wasn't so much about saving money, the money is helpful, but it was more about his families safety- the same family that he left to stay at an old motel.

"Alright Jonny keep an eye on the place I'm headed out," Austin instructed the manager.

"Of course sir." The manager replied with a laugh. The manager then opened the old, rickety door. It screaked forward. He ducked, making sure not to hit his head, walked out and closed the door.

The door slammed shut, enough dust flew to make Austin cough. He walked across the street to his recently purchased building and opened the door with his new keys and stood there looking at all of the work he has to do. Austin opened a new pack of paper towels; he pulls out bags of sponges, cleaning solution, magic erasers and more. He got on his hands and knees and scrubbed floor, the counters, the walls, the place was filthy. Then there was a knock at his door. He answered the door. "Dan! Hey watcha' doing?"

"Nothing man, I just wanted to… come see the …new place. You have your hands full here don't you."

"Yeah, it's gonna take a lot of work."

"I'd say. I'm proud of you though, for starting this up," Dan said, looking around, "but I think that you're kind of starting *big* don't you think? I mean you could have started in your garage or something."

"No, I don't Dan. I think this old building is perfect. It's got what Baz calls charm."

"Well Baz is full of Baz." Dan mumbled. "Austin I'm going to be honest with you, only because I love you like a brother. Why are you wasting your time with this? I mean, you're staying in an old hotel, by yourself, when you've got a nice house and a smokin' hot wife at home. So why are you doing all of this?"

"Because I care."

"About what?"

"The people that this will potentially reach."

"What about your family?"

"What about em'? They're at our new place, you remember the one I told you about, yeah, they're there with everything they need while I work here to get things ready."

"Well, when is the first training or mentoring or whatever you call it?"

"Saturday."

"This Saturday? You have a lot of work to do today my friend. Where'd you get all of this cleaning stuff?"

"Dollar store."

"This isn't going to be easy, but I know that if I wanted to start something like this, that you would be right by my side."

"I would, even if I didn't understand it, that's why we're friends."

"You're right."

"Are you going to help me clean up and stuff?"

"No. actually I have a flight today. I didn't take an extra week off, like you did."

"Oh, ok, well then you better make your flight. Tell everyone that I miss them, and if they get a chance to stop by, and spread the word about Takeoff."

"I will, we are going to miss you."

"I will miss you all too, but these kids are going to need me more than you all will."

"Ok, like I said, I'm not going to fight it anymore. Your wife lost, so... it's no point of me trying to talk you out of it."

"Don't say it like that."

"Don't say it like what Austin? The truth? You gave up your family for this organization."

"My family will be back, as humans we have a few times to make it up to them, but I only have one chance to change someone's life- don't know who it is, I don't know why I'm doing all this, I just know that it's for somebody- somebody will get something out of this program." Austin picked up a broom and began to sweep.

"Austin, Look at me." Austin paused. "You also only have one family, don't lose them. Are they coming Saturday?"

"I don't know...their crazy moma- she's not talking like she wants them to come."

"Well, man, that's not my fight. I wish you the best brother. When are you coming back to work?"

"I don't know, probably next week, I only took one extra week off."

"You're going to be exhausted."

"Yes I will, but you can't be successful and complaining about not getting rest. If you're getting that much rest, then you must not be that busy."

"Well I'm going to go, you have a lot of work to do."

"Ok, send me a lot of pictures from Paris. I always wanted to go there with you guys."

Meanwhile at home…

The doorbell rang. Ashley was still crying a day later from Austin, leaving comes to the door with tissues in hand. "Hi Tyler. How did you find us? Well we don't need you to fix anything anymore."

"I have connections who can find anyone, but you're much to pretty to be crying."

"Oh Tyler, you're a pretty good sweet talker aren't you? My sister is really lucky." Tyler walks in, fixated only on Ashley.

"Yes, yes she is. I'm lucky to have her too."

"So Ashley, Austin really left?"

"Yep, he'll be back, he just needed some space to work on a project."

"*Right.* How are the kids taking it?"

"They think that he just had to go back to work early, so fine for now. We'll resolve things soon."

"Well, you look a little sad, so I want you to come over to my house this weekend. I'll cook for you… we'll joke around… and share some laughs…"

"I don't know."

"Come on, it will help you relax and have a shoulder to cry on. Regina will be there…"

" Ok… fine…Thanks Tyler. I really appreciate it. I'll be there. Tell Regina that I'm coming."

"Austin is really missing out you know? He's letting all of this beauty and perfection go to waste."

"Tyler, you'd better behave yourself. But thanks though, you're sweet. Very- very sweet. My sister is very- very lucky."

Later that evening at the old hotel…

Austin called Ashley. "Hey." Austin said.

"Hey" she said.

"What are you doing?"

"Nothing much"

"Good. I'm coming over to see the kids."

"Ok, but I'm going out. Someone else will be here with the kids."

"You're going out?"

"What, I can't go out now? So you're doing your own thing and leaving me here alone with the kids?"

"Who are you going out with?"

"Does it matter? They won't be home alone, like you left me."

"Don't start this again, Ash."

"Don't you get tired of running across town to see your children? It's not like we are divorced, you could be sleeping in the same bed as me, and wake up every morning and see your kids, but you choose to live in another hotel. You are living a life that people can't stand to live-not with their kids- their wife, and you're living that life for fun."

"Do you think that it's fun to wake up every day, without you next to me?"

"It must be, you seem to be enjoying yourself."
"I'm wearing painter clothes right now, I'm tired, and I've worked all day." Austin said. "See ya' Ash. I gotta go; I'll be over to see the kids in a little bit. Bye."

"Bye."

Austin got in his old car and made his way over to their apartment to see the kids. Austin pulled up to a red light when his phone vibrated on his thigh. "Hello?"

"Captain Jackson? Hi, this is Mr. Sanders…" Mr. Sanders was the quietest man in Dal Airlines corporate headquarters. He was the kind of guy who never left his office or called anyone unless it was absolutely necessary. He was the CEO, but you would never guess that unless you already knew.

"Hey Mr. Sanders how are you?"

"I've been better Mr. Jackson. It has been brought to my attention, that you are putting a lot of time and energy in a non-profit that you're starting?"

"Yes sir I am. I'm just trying to make this happen sir."

"Yes Captain, I understand that, but you are the Senior Captain. And at Dal airlines, your job is not just to fly, but to mentor and impact the younger pilots in the airline. You have meetings and trainings and different activities to go to. I don't see you fulfilling those obligations if you're working as hard as your wife said you are on that nonprofit organization."

"My wife? What did she say?"

"One question, did you leave your family?"

"................yes."

"Captain Jackson, you're not focused on your job. In my book, when a pilot isn't *focused*, people *die*! You are put on administrative leave until you get all of this in your life straightened out. Are you a nonprofit director or are you a pilot? We have never had a plane crash in this airline's 45 year history, and you will not be the first because you're too distracted. Have a good evening '*Mr.*' Jackson"

Austin hung up, tears in his eyes. How could his own wife do this to him? He turned into the drive way. After getting out of the car, he decided something. He decided to pretend. Austin always found peace in acting-pretending that everything was ok- he called this his first heart. Austin always believed that people had three hearts. One that the world can see, one that your closest friends see and one that only he could see. He stood at the door of his house, looked up closed his eyes and took a deep breath. He walked inside. "DADDY!" Mia and Jordan yelled running towards their father. "Hey! What's up buddy? How's everything going?"

"Daddy you're home?"

"I don't know Mia it'll be soon- I promise you." Ashley slowly strolled into the room. Austin looked up at Ashley, feeling Mia and Jordan staring at him. That look was back- admiration- it was a look Austin had seen many times before. It ate away at him- knowing that his children admired him the way they did, yet he was unable to be there for them. "So you guys let me talk to mommy ok?" The kids hugged him, hoping this *talk* would bring him home. They ran up the stairs, "Come on Mia." Jordan called.

"Wait I wanna hear this."

"Hear what?" Jordan said innocently.

"I wanna hear what they're talking about."

"But daddy said go upstairs."

"I know, but I wanna know if he's gonna come home.

"But what about his promise?"

"Jordan, I don't know when you're going to learn… that's just something daddies say."

"I think that you're wrong!"

"Fine then, just listen and see."

Ashley looked at Austin with pain in her eyes-arms crossed and a stern brow. "How's your hotel room?" she said smirking.

"Don't you even do that to me Ash…" He whispered.

"I don't quite know what you're talking about Aus."

"You called my boss today?"

"You know Austin; you told me that you wanted to - *what were your words*? Let you be the head? So go ahead and be the head of your raggedy hotel room."

"Do you know that I was suspended today because of you?"

"Aww, don't you just hate when that happens…" She smirked once more.

"Ash you are unbelievable!" he said walking to the other side of the counter.

"You left the family. I just gave my opinion of why…"

"You know *doggone-well, why.*"

"Well, you thought that it would be a great idea to leave this family and start an *organization.*" She said mockingly.

"You know what!" he walked very closed to Ashley. They were close enough to feel each other's bitterness. "Ashley Jackson, you listen to me, and you listen good, I expect you, and my children- BOTH

Jordan and Mia- to be at Takeoff tomorrow. I don't care about all of that extra. You understand me!? I DON'T CARE! You can call the president of the United States of America, and I don't think I would give a flying *phhh-*"

"-Austin, get out of my apartment."

"*Hey mam*, I don't know if you realized this," Austin said smiling, "But, this is *our* apartment." Austin turned and walked towards the door. He turned to face Ashley, "Have my kids there."

Austin's Journal

I really don't know what is going on in my life right now. My wife is calling my boss and getting me suspended and it's really a big mess. I really close to giving up, but... I can't, for that boy that got shot. For that dream. To change someone's life, and you know the messed up part is that I don't even know who I'm supposed to impact. I guess we'll find out tomorrow... Quick question, am I really that foolish? I feel like a fool. The bills are starting to pile up already and I'm staying at a hotel, spending more money, but now with this unpaid job suspension, money is kinda running tight. I really don't know how long I'll be staying at this hotel...

Chapter 8

Today is the big day. It's an overcast sky and the first session of Takeoff. Five kids showed up; none of them his children. Austin was nervous. He began to introduce himself to the group. "Hi guys." No one said anything. "I said Hi Guys!" there was still a silence. "Hey" one student mumbled. "What's up?" another muttered.

"My name is Captain Austin Jackson, and Welcome to Takeoff." That silence returned. They just stared at him; teenagers are the toughest crowds in America. He continued, "Takeoff is an amazing group. I'm glad that you all are here for the start of it, you guys are going to be like the founding fathers of Takeoff!" They just stared at Austin. Some of them were on their phones texting, some of them were looking at the ceiling, and some of them were looking at their fingernails. "Ok so we're going to get started. Are you guys interested in planes and stuff like that?"

"Yeah, planes... *they aight.*" A student said.

"Good. What's your name?"

"My name is Justin, but they call me JDOG."

"Hey Justin."

"I prefer to be called JDOG man."

"But you said your name was Justin."

"But I prefer to be called JDOG."

"Ok, so you like planes. I think planes are pretty cool. Anybody else like planes?" A few people raised their hands. "What's your name?"

"Ronnie."

"Ronnie? Alright what's up Ronnie?" Another student interrupted Ronnie.

"Well. My granddaddy flew a plane so… that's why I'm here" She said.

"Oh, well since you cut him off, what your name?"

"My name is Justice. And I don't care bout that *lil boy*, I don't care if I cut him off, so what? I'm talking now."

"That's very rude Justice, and that attitude won't get you anywhere."

"You think I care about yo little flight club or whateva?"

"It's not just about Takeoff, it's about wherever you go, or whatever you try to do, that attitude will mess you up."

"I dun heard enough people try and preach to me, ok?"

"Why do you think that all of those people keep preaching to you?" She shrugged her shoulders with an attitude. "Obviously, they care enough about you to waist their air talking to you… So Ronnie tell me what you know about planes."

"I know that they fly high and go far and stuff like that."

"Well Duh, everybody know dat." A student interrupted.

"And what's your name?"

"*My name Paul.*"

"Paul, you like planes?"

"I think that they ok, you know what I'm saying, *they ok.*"

"So Paul what are you going to be when you get older? A pilot, an instructor-what?"

"Naw man, I'm tryna be a rapper." The students laughed at him.

"You're trying to be?" Austin asked.

"Yeah, that's what I'm tryna do with my life."

"Ok, rap a little something."

"Naw man! Don't put me on blast like dat man."

"You know when I was your age, my director used to tell me that you can't say what you *wanna be*, or you're gonna be just that- *a wannabe*." The students laugh. "Alright you guys, so let me tell you about the four forces of flight." Austin starts to draw a plane on the white board. The kids laugh. "Y'all better leave me alone, I know I can't draw." He says joking with them.

"What is that, a deformed bird?" Ronnie said.

"That thang is so ugly." Justice said.

"Hey Capt, I can draw." JDOG said.

"Who said that?" Austin turned around.

"Me. JDOG."

"You can draw, like *for real* draw, not '*play play*' draw?"

"I'm serious Captain, I can draw."

"Yeah me too." Ronnie said.

Justice said, "Well I can't draw."

"Well what are you doing on your phone?" Austin asked.

"Nothing just looking at pictures on Pinstigram."

"Ok... I'm getting an idea. Hi what's your name?" Austin asked the really quiet girl.

"I'm Sarah" She whispered.

"Hi Sarah, what's your talent?" Her next breath unleashed a sound like no other. She started singing. It sounded like a cross between Christina Aguilera and Jennifer Holiday. "WOW." Austin said in shock. "So listen up guys, I have this idea. Sarah and Paul you guys work together to make a song, rap combo about Takeoff. Justice start social media pages on all of the popular sites, and work to get us followers. JDOG and Ronnie are going to make a logo for Takeoff. So everyone lets go, we're going to the store to get some supplies so JDOG and Ronnie here, can make us a cool logo. Everybody in?" The kids cheered. That cheer warmed Austin's heart. This was what all of that hard work was for, this moment. The kids squeezed into Austin's car, and they left Takeoff to go to the arts and craft store.

"Come on *turn up*! Turn up the music Mr. Jackson" Ronnie said.

"I don't do the whole blasting music kind of thing."

"Come on Mr. J don't be lame, come on."

"What's up with you and music Capt? You don't like music? You must be one of those quiet drivers who don't like to listen to music while they drive." JDOG insisted.

"I love music, let me tell you the problem, the problem is that you are an African American. And on top of that you're an African American *male*. Justin-you are judged based on what you wear, how you look, if you're pants are hanging off your behind...So why give anyone something else to talk about by drawing all that unnecessary attention to yourself from blasting your music?"

"Naw man, I'm just an individual, and you know, I'm just trying to express myself. I get what you're saying, but that's not what I'm tryna do."

"It's not even about what you're trying to do Justin. Some things are just the way it is, ok if I take you to a fancy neighborhood right now, and have you blast the music, the first things that's going to happen is they're going to call the police. Then they are going to say to themselves, 'oh how ghetto.' Because that's what I would say if I was living in a real fancy neighborhood. When do you see real successful people blast their music- see Justin you've gotta change your mindset, rappers get paid to act the way they do, but you're trying to act how they act and your broke. Ain't nobody paying you a dime, to act how you acting. Right? It's a mindset, and millionaires they don't act like that, because it's a mentality, like that's the way they think. They can't come home with their music blasting, especially and you're a black young man. Didn't you hear about that guy who got shot because his music was too loud?"

"Man that's… that's just how y'all old people think man."

"Oh, old people, well I'm not that old, but guess what, I didn't get to be this old, and as successful as I am by thinking the way you're thinking."

"WOOOH He got you JDOG, he got you!!" Paul said.

"Justin why do they call you JDOG?" Austin asked.

"That's just what they call me."

"Who is they?"

"You know, some of my friends."

"Who are your friends?"

"You know… some people."

"Some people like a gang?" Austin said looking up in the rearview mirror.

"Well, it's not what you think of when you think of a gang."

"Right I'm sure it's not. What do you guys do? Beat people up? Let me guess it's a whole lot of you guys so who every you're jumping is scared and that makes you guys think that you're bad."

"I mean, we kinda do something like dat, but not how you makin' it sound."

"I'm just kind of saying how it is. That's all. That's what they call you in your gang, JDOG?"

"Yeah, that's where I got it from."

"Interesting…"

"…See man, see… whatchu mean interesting? See, it's people like you who don't *get* people like me."

"I'm a little confused, what's *people like me*?"

"I mean, you all proper and stuff like that. You know, you don't understand that hood life."

"Alright, first of all, you don't me know very well son. I grew up in the hood. I grew up in places where most white people *and* black people are afraid to go. I just learned the secret- that you don't have to reflect the place where you came from. You can come from Bankhead, but act like you came from Buckhead, and who knows the difference? So don't tell me nothing about hood life, I left my family, and am staying at an old, broke down hotel because to save money, so I can keep this organization open. My wife wouldn't even let my kids come today! That's the struggle! And I'm going through all of this because I care so much about each and every one of you."

"But you just met us today." said Sarah.

"You're so right Sarah, but I cared about you guys before I even met you- that's why I started Takeoff."

They arrived at the store. Austin pulled into a space. "Wait Capt… *you left yo fam for us?*"

"Yep. I just see something in you that I want you to see in yourself. That's all. Alright, you guys head into the store get some long paper, paint, rulers, I'll be in the store in a second."

"Yes sir." They said. After Austin's little speech, the kids gained a new respect for him. I think that he knew it, I just think that he was determined to reach JDOG. "Justin! Come with me." Austin quickly reached over to the glove compartment where he had his pistol that he always carries with him for protection. Of course it wasn't loaded, but he took it, and his clip loaded with blanks. He quickly loaded the gun with the blanks and stuffed it in the back of his pants. "Justin come on!" They walk towards the back of the store.

"Man, why don't you call me JDOG man, what's your problem? I'm JDOG, That's my name just call me that it's simple, J- DOG. JDOG!"

"Let me give you the reality, Justin. You want to know why I don't call you JDOG? It's because you're so important. You're important enough for me to call you your real name. You ain't never heard of somebody calling Bill Gates talking about, 'what up B Dog?' he's so important that they have to say his whole name, they don't just say where's Bill, they say where's Bill Gates. So you're so important that I have to say your real name. I'm not calling you your nickname, because *Nick gotta name*. I don't care about what name a gang calls you, alright? It's about time for you to be who you want to be, instead of what someone else wants you to be. I'm telling you, if you become you who were created to be, you're going to be something extraordinary. Now let me talk to you about this little gang that you're in, cause you think that you're a thug." Austin reaches behind him and pulls out his gun. "You think that you're hood, so let me show you what hood looks like." Austin cocks the pistol back. "Let me show you hood little boy!" POW! POW! Austin shot some blanks, and Justin began to cry. "Where's your little gang at? In a real gang you wouldn't ever be walking alone with me. You soft! You walk around with this tough guy image, tryna impress people. You don't impress me!" POW!

"Because I know what thug life looks like, I'm living it!" Austin puts his gun away. He grabs Justin and hugs him. It's alright son, you been trying to be tough for so long, you don't know how weak you are. Leave all of that back here behind this building and be who you were born to be." Justin wipes his face.

"So you live the thug life?" Austin asked, still crying and trying to hold himself together. "You know what, *I do too*: **T**otally **H**umble **U**nder **G**od, the thug life." Suddenly a man walks outside from the back of the store. "WHAT'S GOING ON OUT HERE, I HEARD SHOTS BEING FIRED?!" Austin thought quick, "Yes, someone was out here shooting towards the woods. They made this little boy cry. But don't worry I handled it." The man, who was believed to be the manager, went back inside. "Come on, let's go see what these children want to buy for our logo." They walk inside the store, JDOG dries his eyes and they meet up with the group. "Hey JDOG what do think of these colors man, it's gonna to be sick!"

JDOG responded, "That's nice. That'll be cool. But Ronnie, it's Justin, just Justin." Justin smiled and looked at Austin. This was his vision- making a difference, no matter how crazy the tactics.

Austin's Journal:

I'm going to tell you the truth, I am excited and proud and they are just doing really nice things. I never thought I would be impacting them like this, but they are really awesome. Even little Justice, she's off of her phone and is paying attention now, and the actually did design a logo. I like it, this is it. I'm very proud of them.

Chapter 9

"Alright kids be good for your grandma. I'm going to Mr. Tyler's. Alright, you guys be good!" she yelled upstairs. "Mom I should only be a few hours."

"What are you going to do over there anyway Ashley?"

"I don't know he just wanted me to come over so we can talk about Austin, and the organization, and maybe drink some wine."

"Ooo girl, I don't know, that sounds like a date to me. Isn't that Regina's fiancé?"

"Yes"

"Ok, so does Regina know about this little date?"

"Mom it's not a date. It's just talking with a friend, and she's supposed to be there."

"Well maybe you need to talk to a friend that's a girl, because if I was her I wouldn't be really comfortable with that."

"Well mom, it obviously didn't matter that much to Austin, or he wouldn't have left in the first place."

"You're right, but everything happens for a reason…"

"He already cooked dinner and he's waiting on me. That's the only reason I'm going. Can I use your car? Great! I'll see you in a few hours."

"Ok, I just want you to be careful with that man, I saw him, and he's got a wandering eye. Love you suga"

"Love you too mom."

Austin had been living at the hotel for a week. His deal with the manager was that he would get a discount if he paid per week. Austin spent thousands of dollars on the first Takeoff session- getting tables and chairs, and dry erase boards -getting food, even down to the basics like toilet paper and paper towels.

"Good morning Mr. Jackson, you here to pay for next week?" The manager asked.

"I guess…" Austin sighed. The manager tapped on his computer for a minute then announced, "Ok it will be $75.88."

Austin slowly reached into his pocket and pulled out his credit card. "Yep, just swipe it there." The manager insisted. "Mr. Jackson…" The manager whispered, "It says your card is declined."

"What? That can't be!" Austin proclaimed in disbelief. "Ok, well let's try this one." Austin got out his wallet and took out his debit card. "Now I know this one should work." He said swiping the card. The manager leaned down to whisper again, "Declined sir."

"Declined? I don't understand, how can it be declined?"

"I'm sorry sir I won't be able to help you. Please go collect your things. This is checkout time."

"Wait, hold on let me fix this."

"I'm sorry sir, but when your card is declined once, it's been in my experience that it will continue to be declined, and we need to open up some rooms anyway."

"You don't want my business?"

"Well, honestly sir, it doesn't look like you have any to give me." On that note, Austin turned around and walked to his room. He didn't have much, a few outfits, and some underwear was all he took with from the apartment. He carried his one box out of the hotel, not making any eye contact with the manager. When he walked outside, he saw a tow truck hooking up to someone's car. The car was small, and the truck big so he couldn't see the car, but he thought that that may've been where he parked last night. He slowly walked up to the tow truck.

"Hey man, put my car down!"

"Sorry sir, it'll be $150 here or $250 when I take it back to the yard."

"What? $250! Why am I being towed?"

"Man, you're parked in a handicap space."

"Now if I called the police, you would have to pay that $500 fine."

"Look, I'm sorry. I guess we just got off on the wrong foot." Austin said sitting his box down in front of the tow truck.

"Yeah, you're right, we did." The man held out his hand.

"Austin…. Austin Jackson."

"Mr. Walker." The two shook hands. The tow truck driver continued hooking up the car.

"Wait man, could you please help me? My cards just got maxed out; I don't have anywhere else to go man. Please."

"Sorry sir can't help you." The man tightened his last strap around the tire. He walked around to the driver side and jumped in the tow truck.

"Wait man, come on! Please man! I need help. Come on!" Austin begged. The tow truck sped off, crushing Austin box right in front of it. Austin, still in shock, reached down to get his things. Once he gathered them, walked across the street to his Takeoff building. Once there he noticed a yellow paper on the door. The paper read, FORECLOSURE NOTICE. "Baz!" Austin whispered, "Wait till I see him, he must've done some shady deal, or used some dirty money or something. DANG! *I REALLY CAN'T WIN TODAY!*" He said in disgust. Austin ripped the paper off of the door, and threw it in the box of his things. He opened the door and tossed his box on a table full of bills. Austin took a seat gathering his thoughts. He looked up at the ceiling as his eyes started to water.

His index fingers crossed his lips as if to tell someone to be quiet. He didn't know what to say, or do. Suddenly there was a knock at the door. Austin leisurely walked to the door, still sobbing, sure that it was another bill collector. He opened the door.

"Justin?" He asked.

"Hey Capt. You alright?"

"Yeah, uh, I'm fine. Come on in." Justin walked in the building and quickly scanned the room.

"You know Capt, I been really thinking about our session on Saturday. You really did all of that for us?"

"Yep."

"Wow, man, I just came to say thank you man. I *legit* thought you were bout to shoot me on Saturday, but now I get it. Man, come here." The two hugged. "I feel like I owe you my life man, just for caring as much as you do. That means so much to me man." Justin said in admiration. "Man, yo family must be so lucky." Austin walked over to a chair and sat, wiping his face. "How is your family?"

"Well Justin I don't really know. I've been staying at a hotel for the past week or so."

"Why man? You should be with the *fam*."

"Yeah, you're right, but my wife, she doesn't care about Takeoff, you guys, or anything."

"Capt, I think she does care. Maybe she just has a tough time showing it."

"Well, that's why I left. Excuse me." Austin walked to the restroom leaving his phone on the table. Justin looked around and saw Austin's box of belongings topped with a Foreclosure notice. He sneakily reached over and grabbed Austin's phone. To save money, Austin used a flip phone, so no password was required. Justin flipped the phone open, and went to contacts, and called the one labeled Wife.

"Hello?"

Justin was talking fast, unsure of when Austin would come out of the restroom, "Hello. Hi Mrs. Jackson, you don't know me, but I'm in Takeoff. Your husband has really helped us, and is really making a difference and he's got tons of bills and a foreclosure paper."

"Oh my."

"Ok here he comes, so where can we meet? I have an idea to get your family back together. I know it's none of my business, but he's not looking out for himself, so Mrs. Jackson, I am."

"Alright meet me at the coffee shop on Peter's Street in an hour."

"Ok, I'll be there." Just then, Austin walked out of the restroom.

"What were you doing with my phone?" He asked.

"Well, I couldn't believe how old it was, so I was just looking at it." They laughed. "Well let me go Capt. I got something to do."

"Alright, you better stay out of trouble."

"I will, and Capt, things are about to get so much better."

"I believe it. And pull up your pants boy."

"My bad, I'm still learnin'." Justin pulled up his pants and left. Austin used some paper towels to make a blanket, and took a nap.

The clock struck nine when Austin woke up in a panic. The paper towel blanket was soggy and damp. In the dream his family was being dipped into a pit of lava, and their screams were the only sounds that could be heard for miles. He couldn't save them because he wasn't there. He took that as a sign and gathered his things and ran outside to catch the bus. The mysterious man dressed in black was leaning on the bus stop sign. Austin cautiously walked up to him. "Hey, I've been seeing you a lot lately, how's it going?"

"It's going." The man said.

"What's your name?"

"Tony- my name's Tony."

"Hey Tony I'm Capt- I'm Austin Jackson."

"So Austin, finally I get to have this conversation… do you remember me?"

"I do. I've been seeing you around a lot lately."

"NO! NO! THAT'S NOT WHERE YOU KNOW ME FROM. LOOK ME IN THE EYE AND TELL ME IF YOU REMEMBER ME!" He stared at Austin with a certain look. *His eyes begged for help.*

"Oh my gosh…" Austin stared at him in the eyes, seeing the boy who had been shot when he was six. "It's you."

"YEP IT'S ME. LITTLE TONY. YOU WATCHED ME GET SHOT IN OUR OLD NEIGHBORHOOD!"

"Tony I am sooo sorry. I didn't know what to do. I really didn't."

"I DON'T WANT TO HEAR THAT! I HAD BULLETS REMOVED FROM ME!" Austin put his hand over his mouth in disbelief. "I ALMOST DIED.

JUST A LITTLE SIX YEAR OLD BOY. AND THE MESSED UP PART ABOUT IT IS, I GOT SHOT AND DID NOTHING. I DIDN'T DO ANYTHING WRONG. NOTHING- Just like you. You know the doctors had to use the AED thingy on my three times. He said I had-"

"Three hearts..." Austin interrupted.

"Yes. That's right, but I'm alive and well, and that guy is still on the streets. My parents begged for months on the news for people to come forward."

"I DIDN'T KNOW WHAT TO DO TONY!" Austin yelled. "I was only six, and terrified!"

"When I got out of the hospital, I came to your house to ask you about the shooter, but by then you moved. Convenient."

"What did you want from me? You've got to believe me, you getting shot haunted me until this very day. I felt *so* bad."

"SHUT UP! SHUT UP TALKING TO ME!" he reached into his wallet and pulled out some pictures.

"You see them? Those are my parents. THEY GOT SHOT BECAUSE SOME OF THE SHOOTER'S FRIENDS WERE DARED TO KILL THEM FOR GOING TO THE NEWS!" Tony began to cry. "AND YOU WEREN'T THERE! OUR WHOLE COMMUNITY NEEDED YOU. You… you didn't care about us did you?" Tony pulled out a gun, cocked it back and pressed it on Austin's head.

"Tony can you listen to me? I am so sorry that ignorance killed your parents. That is exactly what I want to change with Takeoff."

"YOU SHOULD'VE WANTED IT 30 YEARS AGO! 30 YEARS AGO YOU DIDN'T WANT ANYTHING. "

"I didn't have all of the answers at that time. I was scared- just a child. Listen if you kill me, you will be just as guilty, just as terrible as the person who shot you and killed your parents. I promise you, I will help you through this, but I need you to put the gun down Tony." Tears flooded his face; he acted like a person with demons fighting inside them. He slowly put the gun down. He walked over to give Austin a hug, then reached in his pocket and quickly pulled a knife. Austin took out his pistol from his back holster. "Tony, drop the knife. I thought you wanted to talk?"

"I do! I just want you to feel the pain I'm feeling right now!" Tony shouted.

Tony assumed a striking pose. His knife hand Lunged at Austin and Austin shot straight between his eyes. Tony flinched, then realized that he wasn't shot. Austin forgot his actual bullets in his towed car. His gun was currently filled with blanks from his encounter with Justin a few days ago. A local patrol cop witnessed the attempted shooting and chirped his siren and flashed his lights. Before Austin realized what was happening he had been taken into custody for attempted homicide. Austin lucked out and was only behind bars for only two hours. Turns out one of the officers was a good friend and was able to get Austin cleared on the charges after things were explained. Tony wasn't dead, after all, and was thankful for being alive. He decided not to press charges, and Austin did the same. He felt like that's the least he could do for the guy- not send him to jail and all.

Austin was taken home by a police friend of his. The officer had his radio on. It was the James Collin's Show, and he had a motivation speaker, the same one Austin heard before. The man instructed the audience, "You should train yourself to feel nothing, because at the end of your feelings is nothing. But if you keep pushing towards your dream, and you put how you *feel* aside, you will succeed." Those few words would save his marriage. Austin arrived at the apartment and desperately wanted to apologize to his wife. "Hey Ms. Margaret."

"Hey Austin what are you doing here?" She asked suspiciously.

"Where's Ashley?"

"She's over at Tyler's… Something about they're having a little get together or something like that over there."

"Ok, well I'm going over there; I need to talk to her!"

"Ok well, I'll be here with the kids then."

At Tyler's house things were heating up…

"Tyler where is Regina?"

"Don't worry she's coming later on…"

"… well I'm going to call her."

"You are so beautiful Ashley. Austin really doesn't deserve you. You're so talented, and funny and fun to be around. I can't believe he would just leave you like that."

"Austin's mom said that everything always works out in the end, but I don't know if I can hold on until the end."

"Well, I tell you this much, if you were mine, I would never treat you that way. I would love you." He got a step closer. "I would care for you." a step closer, "I would hug you." a step closer "And I would just love you to pieces." He grabbed her around her waist. She struggled to back away from him.

"Tyler you are about to marry my sister. You do remember that right?"

"You act like you weren't flirting with me this whole time…"

"Well I was wrong; this boy from Austin's group called me and told me this plan to get our family back."

"Oh yeah?"

"Yeah." Ashley said full of joy. She missed her husband, she was just angry and hurt, but she was still in love with him. "So here's what we're gonna do, we're gonna have this lady at my dance studio, get Austin to come in, meet the lady, and…

"Shh" He put his fingers over her lips. "Why do you put up with all of that with your husband?"

"Because I love him Tyler!"

"Of course, but I also think that you know that I'm the better man for you. And tonight I'm going to prove it."

He held her tightly with one arm and worked to removes his pants with the other, his intentions now clear.

"What are you doing Tyler, put your clothes back on. What's wrong with you?"

Not bothering to knock, Austin barged in and quickly took in the scene. He was unsure of what to think at this point.

His sudden entrance startled Tyler and Ashley was finally able to free herself from his grasp. She ran to Austin and held him tightly, using Austin as a shield. "What are you doing here?" she stammered, quickly followed by "I'm so glad to see you!"

"You stay away from my wife!" he warned Tyler. "And while you are at it, stay away from Regina too. She doesn't need scum like you, and you don't deserve her." Austin pulled out his pistol, given back to him by the police department, "And that is the final warning."

He shut Tyler's door, and walked to Margaret's car and faced each other.

"I'm glad that you didn't do anything."

"I was never going too. I just wanted to talk, that's all. We were just friends. Or so I thought. You know I love you."

"And I you. I've decided that I will be coming home, tonight- for good."

Back at home Ashley told her mom what happened over at Tyler's house. "Can you believe he did that mom?"

"Yes, I really can. Didn't I warn you? I told you not to go over there. At least you are safe now." They hug. Then Ms. Margaret turns to Austin "Anyway, how's Takeoff going?" She asked spitefully. Ashley added her voice to the question. "Yeah baby, let's talk about Takeoff."

"Well, it's really taking off. One of the kids, I had to threaten him with a gun. He's a gang member. They call him JDOG, and he said, 'how come you don't call me JDOG?'" They laughed and laughed about that story. Austin told more of his stories about those crazy kids at Takeoff.

"Austin, why do you spend so much time with Takeoff? Are they more important than your own family? I want us to spend time together, as family, or just ourselves." Ashley said.

"Why not? I'll go to work with you tomorrow."

"You teach on Sundays?" Margret interrupted.

"Yes mom, sometimes." She turned back to Austin. "But you're going to come for real?"

"Yep I'll be there until you leave."

"I would love that! You know something, you really are good with those kids from Takeoff. I'm proud of you, and I'm sorry that I couldn't see that vision."

"I'm sorry that I wanted you to sell the house."
They laughed. "We are a crazy couple aren't we?"

"Yep, but we work. I don't know how but we
do."

The next day...

"Come on ladies, do it one more time, five, six-
five- six- seven-eight. This lady, about 4 foot 11, stares
at Austin from across Ashley's dance studio. She was
an older white woman, faded dyed hair, perfume that
you could smell when she got out of the car... She
stared for about 30 minutes. "Alright girls, let's take
five- you did good!" Ashley said with enthusiasm.
The lady took that as an opportunity and began to
walk over. "Hi there I'm..."

"Yes I know who you are, you're Sava Ringgold.
How are you?" Sava Ringgold is one of the richest
women in Atlanta. She is also one of the most
generous philanthropists and is a huge advocate of
youth leadership, and Austin knows this.

"I'm doing fantastic. The other mothers tell me that you have a youth program?"

"I do it's called Takeoff. It's a youth mentoring company-well organization, it's a non-profit.

"It's centered around aviation. I love flying—I am a pilot you know—and I figure if I can get kids interested in aviation somehow, keep them busy at Takeoff, then I can keep them off the streets, and hopefully make a difference in the meantime."

"Mmmhmmm." Mrs. Ringgold nodded approvingly. "Is this organization of yours strictly for troubled youth, young man?" She queried.

Austin was taken by surprise. He honestly had only thought of the troubled youth from the hood. He wasn't sure where this conversation was leading. "So far, Mrs. Ringgold, I only have troubled youth in the group." He was stalling for time as new ideas formed in his head. "But I don't see why it should matter. In fact, having a wide range of children attending would not be a bad idea. Some of these kids need positive influences in their lives, and sometimes it may not hurt children who are better off to see how other kids struggle with thing they take for granted." Austin was amazed at what he was saying. It was like he was having an epiphany, right there in front of the richest woman in Atlanta. He hoped he hadn't said the wrong thing.

The air was dead silent for a moment. A moment that lasted a lifetime. A pin dropping would cut the silence like a gong.

Finally she spoke. "Very well, Mr. Jackson. The other mothers speak highly of you and Takeoff. They tell me how you have struggled to make it work, and how it is making a difference their children's lives. "I would like to have my daughter join your organization."

Austin was taken by complete surprise. Afraid of saying the wrong thing, or of just simply stuttering, he paused a moment to collect his thoughts.

"I don't know what to say, Mrs. Ringgold. I would be honored to have your daughter join."

"It is settled then."

Austin could only imagine what this may mean to the other kids. But, knowing the kids from the hood, there was no way of knowing if him making such a hasty decision was a good or bad thing.

Mrs. Ringgold continued, "Mr. Jackson, I just want to let you know, I have 5 million dollars I would like to donate somewhere. I may have just found that place."

Austin nodded. He knew what she was saying. If she continues to like what she sees, Takeoff would get the donation. She continued once more, "I feel Takeoff is the best thing I've heard of in a long time...

... I love the whole aviation thing, and the leadership aspect of it, and your personality sells it alone and dedication to other people's children- to make them better- then have to go home to your own children- I can only imagine! That says a lot about you Mr. Jackson. Takeoff will go very far, I promise you that Mr. Jackson!" Austin looked over Mrs. Ringgold and saw Ashley, Justin, and Dan waving at him in the background. At that moment he knew that she was planted there, for him to meet. He was filled with such joy. Not only was receiving a 5 million dollar investment, but his beautiful wife, his mentoree and his best friend were all finally seeing the vision of Takeoff.

Chapter 10

1 year later...

One evening coming home from a Takeoff benefit dinner, Austin and Ashley decided to take a trip back down memory lane. "Can you believe that we came from that to where we are now? I mean we sold that old building that *we*, well, *I* foolishly bought for 500,000 dollars, and now I lease it out. Takeoff Non Profit collapsed allowed us to combine it with your dance company, and you were gracious enough to let me call the new company Takeoff Incorporated," Austin drove toward the old Takeoff headquarters.

"I know" Ashley replied.

"Ash now we operate out of a three story 50,000 square foot building, and have over 1,500 members, and we've just expanded so much over the past year." Austin proclaimed full of ambition. Ashley interrupted, "I know. Now we focus on aviation as method to channel their leadership skills, as well as flying. The merger of my dance company allowed us to add dancing,"

"And don't forget the Karate we added for self-defense, and cooking for self-reliance," Austin chimed in. "Just think, we came from a broke non-profit to now bringing in revenue over $11 million each year."

Ashley added. "And you are the big dog himself, Mr. CEO."

Austin chuckled. "Nah, I'm not the big dog. That would be JDog I mean, Justin. He and Ronnie help out with the marketing. Who woulda' thought?"

"You lucked out mister. You were in the doghouse big time. First you buy that run down building for an ungodly price, then you sell our home and force us to live in a dinky apartment—not to mention, you sold my car right out from under me!"

"Hey," Austin replied quickly, "What are you complaining about? We've got the new place in the country, complete with a big yard and a pool for the kids. And you got your dream car."

"Yeah, and you got yours." They both were quiet for a few moments as each reminisced about the ups and downs they had over the past year.

"Regina left Tyler and now works as a receptionist for Takeoff Inc…"

"Yep and she should've. She deserves better."

"Yeah, she does, but did I tell you how she dumped him?"

"*No*- what she do?"

"She took him to a park, 30 miles outside of town, and made him get out and walk home."

"That's all? I thought you were going to say, she poured some hot grits on him, or set his grass on fire or something crazy like that…" Austin said chuckling.

"…Yeah, well, for Regina, that's as bad as it gets- having to walk." She laughed.

"You're wrong for that one…" Austin laughed.

Ashley suddenly sprang up. "Hey babe, what happens to the original members? I feel like we should give them something, because when you think about it, without them we wouldn't have all of this.

Yeah, I think I'll give them full scholarships to wherever they want to go to college. We have the money now.

"I KNOW!" She laughed. "But don't get me started, because you shouldn't have left the family and went all crazy and bought this building in the first place."

"I know." Austin said looking down.

"But… I'm glad you did leave us to do this. This old building got us to where we are now. Plus I can admit that there were some things that I shouldn't 've done either."

"Uuummhuumm."

Ashley started crying, "…And I never really told you how sorry I was for that! And you not once questioned it…"

"I love you too much." He looked at her and grabbed her hand, and kissed it gently. "So how about me and you get some *alone time* when we get home, and then bask in our success…" Austin got out of the car to stare at the old building where it all started, Ashley followed.

"Yeah, baby I would love too, but…"

"…But we really owe it all to God. Think about it we wouldn't be millionaires if we didn't go through this and see through the clouds and the rough times when it was hard to see…"

"… So true, but baby, God has been even better to us than we thought…"

"… Yeah I know, he does things *way* beyond our wildest dreams, doesn't he…"

"… Yep, and I knew you'd be excited and what better place to tell you how good God has been, we're having another baby!" Ashley squealed in excitement.

"Yep… wait what? Seriously?" Austin's face lit up. His smile went from ear to ear.

"Yes! I'm so excited. I just don't know what to do!" She threw herself into his arms.

"Oh my goodness Ash… wow… a baby… hold on somebody's calling me."

"It's probably my mom; you know she gets tired of watching the kids around eleven p.m. Then she's just ready to go home." Ashley chucked still mentally celebrating her pregnancy.

"Oh it's *my* mom, that's weird." He swiped the screen to answer his phone, "Hello? Yes… ok…

when? Now? Wait… mom… slow down… mom… I… Hello? Hello? Mom!?"

"What's wrong?"

"I don't know, my mom's freaking out- asking questions about when was the last time I talked to dad, and stuff like that."

"Oh boy, we better get over there and see what's going on." Austin and Ashley ran back to the car.

"Yeah, call your mom and tell her what's going on. Tell her it'll be a minute. Tell her I'll pay her extra, I just need to go and see what's going on."

"Ok." He started the car up, and sped away.

Arriving at Danielle and Russ' house the neighborhood was strangely quiet, and peaceful. The sky was clear and it was a full moon out this night. Austin and Ashley ran up to the door, it was open. They walked in and the atmosphere completely changed. Danielle ran up to Austin to hug him. "Oh son! I'm so glad you're here." She said in between her tears. "What's wrong mom?"

"It's your father."

"Yeah, what about dad?"

"Go look in the next room son…" Austin slowly and carefully glided to the next room. He didn't know what to think on his short walk to the next room. He was a bit confused, a bit disorientated. He was just happy about the baby, and now he doesn't know what he'll find in the next room.

He slowly turns the corner. On the bed was Russ, pale, staring at the ceiling, mouth open- dead. Austin instantly broke down. He prepared himself for the worst, but didn't think this was the worst. He breaks down in tears. He screams, "WHY?! WHY?! WHAT WOULD MAKE YOU TAKE MY FATHER!?" His mom walked in, looking at the floor, terrified of looking at Russ on the bed. She told Austin, "Come on baby, come on. 911 was called, and they are on the way."

"Mom he's not dead is he? He can't be!" More tears flowed from his eyes. He hadn't cried this much in his separation from his family, or his unborn child, but the death of his father was simply too much for him. The remainder of that night was a blur. Austin had gone into some state of shock. He didn't see or hear anything. He only could see his father lying on the bed. Once his father was taken away by the coroner, Austin and Ashley took Danielle home with them. She was crushed. Just like Austin, Russ was her rock. The foundation of her new sobriety- her life- everything. At Austin's house Danielle decided she needed some rest, and cried herself to sleep. For the rest of the night, Austin sat in his home movie theatre, accompanied by his wife and children, and they watched old videos of his beloved father and their grandfather, until they all fell asleep... except of course, Austin.

Epilogue:

At a press conference for Takeoff Incorporated, all of the press was there. Austin's mother was there dressed in black. Sitting behind him on the stage, were his now 3 children: Jordan, Mia, and his new baby boy, Russell and his wonderful wife Ashley.

"Good Evening. I would like to first thank all of you for coming. I will try my best to make this as short and simple as possible." The crowd chuckled and Austin smiled. "Takeoff Incorporated was built from a passion for leading young people to greatness. In fact, that's our slogan. We have many departments which enrich today's youth by finding whatever their passion is and building on it. I thank Mrs. Ringgold for believing in Takeoff, and believing in me enough to invest in the program. That is the reason all of us are here. Years ago, more like decades, I went to a private school called Foundation Christian Academy. They had a saying, 'Leadership starts with a foundation.' It is that saying and that philosophy that has *'Trail-blazed'* the fundamentals of Takeoff. I would like to thank those who were a part of that school, for making me who I am today. I would also like to thank my JROTC program back in high school. See, once the foundation was laid, JROTC build on it. The South Fulton Arrow Youth Council used what JROTC built, so that I would be able to do what I am doing today. Thank you for that. I would also like to thank my family, for supporting me- even through the rough times- and being patient with me while I've been busy working with other people's children. My family is a major factor in Takeoff's success.

As many of you are aware, my father Russ Jackson, an engineer for over 30 years, died about 3 months ago. I would like to thank all of you for your condolences and prayers. While reading bereavement cards and thanking the senders of those cards, I was busy at work, to make my Father's legacy one that will never go out. A brain aneurism took him away from us in flesh, but never from our hearts. It is with that, that I would like to announce the open

enrollment for Takeoff's new engineering program."
The audience applauded. "This program will be
offering a scholarship called the Russ Jackson
Memorial Scholarship. The winner of each year will
receive a full scholarship to any college or university
in the nation!" The audience stood to their feet and
applauded. Austin's family stood to applaud.
Austin's mom cried, perhaps tears of joy and sorrow.

"So if you take anything away from this speech,
or my life, or my story, ladies and gentlemen- take
away that if you keep doing the right things, for the
right reasons, it will pay off, and you will succeed, or
as we call it *Takeoff*.

Put in the work, put in the time, and the blood,
sweat and tears, but do it for the right reasons
because:

Galatians 6:7 "… a man reaps what he sows."

James 3:18 "Peacemakers, who sow in peace, will
reap in righteousness."

Other Recognitions and Special Thanks:

J'Lynne Jordan

Ashley Dozier

Keith L. Brown

Pastor Maya Taylor

Thank you all for your wonderful words of motivation. These words have led to greatness.

A note from the author:

Thank you for taking the time to read my story Takeoff: Seeing Beyond the Clouds. I certainly hope you enjoyed reading it as I did writing it. Please visit Lulu.com, Amazon.com or barnsandnoble.com and leave me a brief review.

Thank you,

Austin Jackson

Special Thanks to Hazen Wardle, the author of The Triumph Detective, for assisting me and helping me get this masterpiece ready for the world to see it.

Do you like cool hats, shirts, phone cases and more?

Visit the Takeoff Superstore at:

Takeoff.spreadshirt.com